I0541025

Blue Princess:
The Storybook Planet

A Science Fiction Novel in the
Empire of Time Series
by
John Argo

Clocktower Books, San Diego

Blue Princess: The Storybook Planet
Copyright © 1973, 1997 by John Argo. All Rights Reserved.

—This novel, which I wrote at age 23, was originally titled *The Storybook Festival*. It did not see light of publication until 1997 under the title *Pioneers*. It joined the other six novels currently part of my *Empire of Time* series. After putting it through several editions in online and indie publishing, I have retitled it Blue Princess: The Storybook Planet as a hybrid of past, enduring themes in the novel. The Blue Princess, Auska, is a key player in the life of Pioneer Paul Menard and among the aboriginal people of the Storybook Planet (N-60A). It all makes story sense.
—Cover images sourced from stock photo services including iStock, Fotolia, and FotoSearch. The owners of the photos reserve all rights to their intellectual property, which Clocktower Books paid to use.
—Clocktower Books, a San Diego small presss, and early Internet publisher, continues its pioneering tradition: "Exciting Books for Avid Readers on the Web Since 1996"

I chose the pseudonym John Argoin 1996 when publishing the world's first HTML novel online (*Neon Blue*). It reflects the sense of wonder we felt at the pioneering team of Clocktower Books about the infinite possibilities and promise of digital and online publishing. Argo was the ship of wonder in ancient Bronze Age stories, when the Argonauts (literally, Argo-Sailors) sailed forth into deep space of their time (the Aegean and Pontic Seas). Among their timeless adventures, still told in movies today, was the quest for the Golden Fleece.
—Snail-Mail Contact:
Clocktower Books
P. O. Box 600973
Grantville Station 92160
San Diego, California 92160-0973
—E-Mail Contact: Editor/Publisher
editorial@clocktowerbooks.com
You can find us online at www.clocktowerbooks.com

1. New World—Year 3301

The crash landing on N60A jarred Paul Menard's teeth and mauled him around in his web seat. It wasn't his spouse Licia's flying nearby in the pilot seat, but the thousand-year sleep from which the ship and the last six surviving humans had just awakened. Would computer programs written a millennium ago work? The ancient code had been written on a dying Earth, choking in clouds—like a new gas giant, on a smaller scale, but just as toxic and deadly—by programmers and engineers who were by now long dust and forgotten.

Far from the now lost Earth, the last six human pioneers were making their hard landings on the alien world that was mankind's last and only hope for survival. At the moment, smashed around in a blur so that his teeth rattled and his eyes dimmed, Menard's only thought was of surviving through the next few seconds.

Then they could worry about their fresh, sweet, green new home with its flowing rivers and blue skies, its oxygen-rich winds and tiny birds unlike the giant, evolved raptors terrorizing ancient Earth's high cloud deck.

For the moment, the game was just survival—from second to second.

And Paul Menard wasn't sure if he was about to die, or step outside into a wonderful new world that had been promised by enticing radio messages from the advanced civilization of N60A, an Earth-like planet orbiting a yellow sun much like old Sol.

In the other cockpit seat, Paul's spouse Licia screamed once, briefly, as she lost control of the craft she had piloted down from orbit.

The lifeboat bounced and scraped wildly across alien grasslands.

For minutes that seemed like hours, Paul faced the terrifying vision of his own imminent death as the boat yawed right and left, smashing through trees at the beginning of a forest.

Everything was a blur as the big boat rocked up and down, slamming against rocks and trees on its final trip through a forest and down into a canyon

Paul closed his eyes and prepared for the final slam into death.

But the boat came to a sickening stop amid boulders and trees.

In the eerie silence, Paul opened his eyes. He was grateful for the heavy-duty web straps that had held him down and probably saved his life. The cabin was filled with a fine gray haze through which the panels of instruments and scattered green, red, and amber lights were difficult to see.

Through the blood dripping from his nose, Paul smelled smoke. He'd deal with that in a moment. The lights were going out around him. The control panels were going dark one after another as he anxiously reached out to feel his spouse's pulse. In the oppressive silence, Licia's petite body lay in the pilot chair. Her head lay turned to one side from the shock of impact. The air recirculator system was out, and the air was still and suffocating as in a tomb. He feared the worst, but was relieved to feel a strong pulse. "Licia!"

Paul smelled a thickening smoke and recognized the boat truly was on fire—his other worst nightmare.

He undid his straps and jumped from his seat. Raising his arms to the ceiling, he slammed his palms one by one down the line against the double row of square red plaques that should activate the ship's fire-fighting controls—no response. This lifeboat was on fire, and it could no longer protect itself or its precious cargo: the entire recorded history, and one third of the survivors, of the human race.

He and Licia were 25 light years from home after a thousand year sleep, during which Earth and all its remaining people had perished. There was no way back. Licia had piloted well during the descent from the orbiting mother ship, headed for a mirror-bright lake. The plan was to touch down on the lake surface, braking, and then come to a gentle rest against its muddy shores. A sudden loss of power had put an end to that plan, and forced them down among the uneven green hills.

"Come on!" he yelled, shaking Licia. The lights were going out around him. The control panels one by one went dark. An acrid taste of smoke was in his mouth. It stung his nose despite the rag he held there to staunch the bleeding. The dead viewing screens all around were dark and blind. The corridor behind was getting cloudy. "The whole circus will go up at any second! If that doesn't get us, we'll die of smoke inhalation."

While she rose unsteadily, he ran down the corridor through roiling smoke and, putting his back to the wall, kicked the escape hatch open. The smoke's muddy, yellowish color suggested toxic insulation burning. It was an electrical fire for now; at any moment it could flash through and ignite the whole craft.

"The library!" Licia yelled, coughing, as she stumbled down the corridor lugging bulky emergency equipment with many trailing straps. Both he and she wore loose fitting gray jumpsuits; no time to even recover their bubble helmets! Licia dropped an armload of dark military-looking satchels and waved a hand before her eyes and nose. Then she pulled the blue canvas weapons bag from its wall holder and tossed it out of the boat. "The library!"

"Can't save it!" he yelled. He could barely see her as he reached for her. He had a last glimpse of the interior—a hundred foot ship that could have made a comfortable home. It had a complete library of now-dead Earth's knowledge—the stuff needed to start a new civilization without having to repeat the first 5,000 years or more. Thank God there was redundancy—the other two lifeboats had libraries, as did the mother ship, which was scheduled to orbit the planet for thousands of years. Where were the other two lifeboats? Hopefully the other two pioneer pairs were making a better landfall.

Paul jumped the bone-jarring ten feet down along the lifeboat's featureless sides. Gravity seemed about right. Paul felt his breath squeezed out as his knees slammed against his chest. Stunned and aching, he turned to help Licia, but she had already jumped free, holding backpacks with flailing straps in each arm. "Quick!" they both yelled at the same time.

Paul picked up the weapons satchel even as Licia rose from her stumble. She tossed one of the packs, he caught it, and they both ran.

Man and spouse struggled uphill through thick underbrush, burdened by heavy packs.

Their breathing was ragged and desperate, but in a way glad because they were alive—the last hope of an Earth now forever barren of human life. A warm yellow sun pierced the immense, oxygen-rich sky. Two moons, one silver and the other white, formed wan crescents on the horizon. If they could just get over the—.

The wreckage of their lifeboat glinted at the foot of the hill in the edge of a seemingly endless green-brown forest full of life. The ship began to make loud banging sounds. Some of that was ammunition going off. Some of it was fuel tanks rupturing. Thick black smoke poured like liquid from the open hatch and from the broken exhausts under the stubby wings.

Survive, a thing said inside Paul, *conquer*. He thought of his mentor SheuXe, and nodded grimly. This world was going to be theirs, no matter what the cost. In Licia's tired eyes and mussy hair he read the same determination. After a thousand-year sleep, they had got here and it was a lovely world, not at all the coal-black hell of freezing ammonia storms or worse they might have feared. Mysteries, though: seen from orbit, random campfires, ruins. Not the wonderful galaxy-spanning civilization that had advertised itself across the light-years. Instead, ruins.

From the top of the hill, they would search for the other two lifeboats; the other two men and two women; the rest of the human race.

A four-winged bird rested in a headwind high up.

Two figures scrambled up the alien hillside: Paul anxious to reach the top and holding Licia's hand; she stumbling as he pulled her along.

The lifeboat exploded. Its skin tore, and a cloud roiled up hundreds of feet.

The blast knocked Paul and Licia flat on the hilltop, deafening them.

He threw himself over her as thousands of tiny shards rained down for a full minute.

If a big piece hit one of them, it would be all over.

He closed his eyes, feeling her wiry strength and feminine softness under him, loving her; and yet he still felt that tiny bit of resentment.

She was, after all, and would always be, Alicia Krings.

A thousand years ago, he had stolen her from the house of her father, automatically imposing a death sentence on the elder Krings under harsh, implacable Aerie laws.

In the close Aerie quarters, the surviving humans on earth had to live in oppressive proximity with each other.

Krings knew he was doomed.

Paul was gripped with a deathly resolution to explode from the cramped Aerie, and escape into open space.

The last flight out from Earth could not come soon enough.

As the pieces of the boat rained down on the grass and trees of this alien new world, he thought of Krings, dead now 1,000 years.

Paul wondered if he and Licia would share the same fate in the next few seconds.

2. Old World—Year 2299

Paul Menard rested his cheek against thick glass as he and Master Engineer Roger Krings sat deadlocked in their debate of survival priorities.

The own grim situation would never come up in conversation. Each had thought of killing the other in a duel, and each had let the thought go, knowing Licia would not sanction it.

The Rocky Mountain Aerie window overlooked angry black cloud cover obscuring the bitten, stunted landscape of Earth. Muffled thunder regularly growled in the electrically tormented clouds below. As the mountains rolled into dusk, the evening sun shone into the small turret room where Paul often came to sit alone. Even in the remaining aeries, populations were dwindling and one could find many places to be alone—too many. Only today he was not alone.

Startled by a noise minutes ago, he'd turned.

Roger Krings stood in the doorway, award-rich and much honored, but now in danger of being despoused. Paul was about to take his daughter from him, his remaining woman, and under Aerie law that meant Krings must be put to death. Spousing didn't mean you slept with each other; it meant any man-woman relationship. When you became despoused, they disposed of you. That was Old Law, of course, when there had been too many people. Now it was nothing like that, but the old shame remained. Krings would be allowed to remain in his spacious condominium, close to the precious earth, but there would be a stigma. Without meaning to, or knowing why, people would dread speaking with him. They would shun the formerly great man. He would probably step outside one day—he'd all but threatened this, in an effort to keep Licia with him—having said goodbye to his few remaining contacts. He had no students any more. He would step outside without benefit of suit or helmet and pick his way down the old U.S. Forest Service trail. Probably cold would kill him first. If he chose to wear thick clothing, he'd go a bit farther down until the air delivered less oxygen to his laboring lungs. If he wore breathing pack and helmet, he might make it almost to the shores of the mysterious sea. Before the comets had rained down, before the Earth had vomited up slag and smoke, the sea had already risen to new highs and made new beaches. That was generations ago. It was pitch dark down there, people said—no one had gone there and returned alive—but robot probes suggested strange things living down there that relished the poison air, and glowed greenish-yellow when excited. If nothing else got him, these things would.

"Well, Conquering Hero, you are about to lift your wings."

Paul, two weeks away from launching, looked away.

"I came to talk about Licia," Krings said perspiring.

"We have talked enough about it." Paul sweated but felt cold. He coughed gently and looked out of the window. Two condors, faint dots at first, approached high over the alternating black patches and white-and-gold angel's hair clouds. Krings too had noticed, and bent at the knees to watch.

The condors tangled briefly, losing altitude. When they had nearly sunk into the cloud tomb, they abruptly parted by truce of mutual necessity. They climbed steeply upward and apart.

"The new kind," Krings said scientifically.

The leading condor passed over the buttressed gray Aerie walls like a shadow, its wing span over 100 feet. The birds were thickly insulated with fat and feathers. They could lift a dog or a child into the upper atmosphere within minutes, to suffocate their prey. As the birds passed, their shadows flitted over the Aerie, each shadow for an instant darkening the room.

Krings began to blubber.

3. New World—Year 3301

After the lifeboat's explosion, objects rained down banging loudly on the hillsides around them. One crumpled sheet of fuselage sailed down, landed on its side, and rolled before keeling over with a soft sound. The air smelled of burning plastic. A plume of black smoke rose, and the boat continued to burn loudly and vigorously, but objects stopped falling. The danger was over—that danger, anyway.

A small lacy-winged butterfly flew along the crest of the alien hilltop, buffeted in spiraling motions by the gentle, erratic wind.

Paul released Licia's hand and threw himself on his belly, panting. Licia dropped beside him. Her pale delicate face was flushed and scratched, and her light-brown hair was full of tiny vegetal debris, but her eyes were flinty and determined. She was, he thought, a stronger personality than her father had been. No wonder SheuXe had overruled the Council about forcing her to stay with her father. It had been a matter of which was the greater work—to save the Aerie, which Krings purported to be doing by his new solar oxygenator, though the cynic Souspolitis and other critics publicly denied it; or to send her to help found a new humanity elsewhere, which the cronies of Krings had loudly derided in Council. Those had all been words, spoken far away and long ago, on a planet that was inexorably turning into an initially more watery variation of its neighbor Venus.

Paul scanned with binoculars, "All I see is flat land. Some buffalo, I think, grazing. Clusters of trees. Water in small, shiny pools." They had a rifle, one sidearm, one long all-purpose knife. Each also carried a compass and canteen in addition to a heavy backpack.

Licia drank deeply from her canteen and wiped her mouth with her sleeve. "It smells wonderful here. Can you smell the plants? The grass?" They gazed across the quiet wind-combed plains so beautiful and eerie, acutely aware, as every child learned in school, that once upon a time the Earth itself had been a storybook planet like this.

"Bovis whatsis," she mused, staring through the binocs. The powder-blue sky was exhilarating. On impulse, he embraced her. She bent close to kiss him. He laughed, rolling over onto his back, and wrestled with her. Good aerie-dwellers, they knew from long ago that there must be laughter even at the most sad or dangerous times.

A faint whistling noise came from high up.

Paul heard it, felt Licia freeze in his arms as they both turned their gaze upwards.

On the plains below, several buffalo rose. Others pawed the ground nervously. The whistling grew in intensity, deepening to a roar.

"The mother ship," Paul said.

"Oh no!" she wailed. Her gaze followed the direction of his pointing finger.

High up, a thin white trail had fallen out of space. As they watched, it lengthened its downward curve.

"No!" Paul echoed.

"The trajectory must have been off slightly. It's being pulled into the atmosphere," Licia said. At its tip was a tiny dot of intense light. The derelict spaceship, which had brought them from Earth while they slept a thousand-year sleep, was about to fall from the sky. It appeared headed directly toward them.

"Another library lost," he protested, thinking of all the stored knowledge of thousands of years of human history about to fry in a brief display of thunder and light. "All those media are duplicated in the two remaining lifeboats, waterproof and so on; whoa, but here she comes!"

High up, a thin thread had fallen out of space. Paul wrapped his arms about Licia, burying her under him. A wide swath of steam trailed across the sky. At its forefront was the glowing, still uninflamed derelict. Any second now—there! She lit like a match, glowed like a pale moon, crossed the sky, making buffalo suddenly bolt as one. The sound was that of a gigantic plow being dragged scraping and screeching across the floor tiles of Olympus. The alien world trembled briefly. A small lacy-winged butterfly flew along the crest of the alien hilltop, buffeted in spiraling motions by the gentle, erratic wind. The next instant, a hovering hawk-like raptor—shimmering greenish feathers on top, thick brown fur below—

plunged, snapping up the butterfly in one gulp, before climbing with innocent laziness back toward survey altitude.

Paul closed his eyes and held Licia close, remembering how, in her desperation to escape her father's suffocating grip on her, she'd come to seduce him, a millennium ago, a thousand revolutions of that poisoned cloud-planet the Earth around its sun, no longer their home now, but in those days still affording humanity a few tenuous toe-holds in the high mountains. He remembered his first close view of her, right after the condor games.

4. Old World—Year 2299

A knock sounded at the door of his one-bedroom apartment in the upper Aerie. Paul rose from bed wearing his robe, and holding a half-full glass of scotch and tinkling ice cubes. Plans for a proposed interstellar mission, two years in future if it were to happen at all, were scattered across the bed. Among them lay a heavy, wide-mouthed black rifle he had been absently cleaning and oiling: A condor gun.

Opening the door, he stared. She!

He had seen her for the first time at the bird-baiting games two days earlier. It wasn't the first time he'd seen her, actually. The Aerie still had nearly 20,000 inhabitants, down from 45,000 fifty years earlier. There were a hundred aeries around the world, all in mountainous regions. Each supported 2,000 to 50,000 inhabitants. In all, about a million humans remained from a pre-doom population of up to ten billion. The Rocky Mountain Aerie was one of the largest. It sprawled over dozens of acres in an area known long ago as New Mexico. It had several schools, several shopping malls as they were still known, hundreds of businesses. It was possible for two persons to rarely ever see each other. Then again, it was possible for two persons one day to stare at each other as though it were for the first time, and to see each other as they never had before.

Paul had been pike man in the games. His partner had been Robert Tynan, a brilliant young engineer. Both men wore blue jumpsuits that insulated against the cold while allowing free range of motion. The only weapons in the game were a club and a ten-foot spear, or pike, with a razor sharp steel point. Tynan's job, as clubman, had been to bring the bird in, as a matador might long ago have taunted a bull. These giant birds were not at all shy, and not easily frightened. After all, since the radical shift in the ecology, the upper atmosphere had become the secure spot in the food chain, and they were the kings of that domain. This bird, a black King Condor with a wing span of 30 or 35 feet, was hungry. Its beak was serrated for killing, and those claws were scarred from fighting other denizens of the air. Tynan, a strapping man of athletic physique and stubborn courage, had gone out on the bare, snowy tarmac holding his club. The trick in this part of the game was not to be too far from the bait nor too close. The bait was a mewling lamb and its mother. The lamb fretted about their small fenced in area while the mother stood stoically. Already, black shadows crept in front of the sun. Raspy cawing traveled for miles in the brilliantly blue sky as the birds talked to one another in a setup for the attack. Paul watched carefully, pike ready to go to Tynan's assistance if necessary. Sure enough, there came their antagonist, a good-sized alpha male from a flock that roosted on a nearby mountain top. The Hunt Club would be dining on lamb, mutton, and fowl tonight, Paul thought with grim pleasure. Since Gregory, he hated the birds.

The helos had been stored below. Above on the rampart, several hundred spectators watched, bundled in heavy clothing. Their features were mostly unrecognizable, muffled by scarves and wool hats. The bird settled slowly, wings noisy in the thick air. The trick was for him to go for the sheep, not for Tynan. Sure enough, as the crowd screamed and hooted, the bird looked from one to the other and raced across the snow with wings pointed up, headed straight for Tynan. Tynan turned to run, but fell. What should have happened was that the bird would go for the sheep, and Tynan would run up and club it across the head. As it lay momentarily dazed, he would slip a noose around its leg, anchoring it to the ground. Then the pike man, in this case Paul, would run out and with great showmanship duel the bird to its death. Or, as sometimes happened, his own. Then it was the custom to shoot the bird and hang its head on the rampart as a ghoulish tribute for the other birds to peck at.

The bird was upon Tynan. Paul ran, readying the pike as he went. The bird managed to gash Tynan's clothing, which was thickly insulated; no blood appeared on his torso. The bird suddenly looked up, aware of Paul running toward it. Its eyes contained 120 million years of evolutionary mercilessness and survival pride. In that moment, Tynan swung the club. His swing was weakened by his position on his back, with the bird's claws on his leg, but he caught it awkwardly across the face. It darted back, without relinquishing its hold on him, and snapped its beak to one side. The club flew away. Paul ran at full tilt, bringing the pike back like a throwing spear—something never seen before, but the moment was desperate—and lunged. The composite shaft whirled through the air, penetrating the bird's neck. The condor backed up, flailing angrily, making the wound worse. Scarlet jelly ran down its chest and spattered the snow. There hadn't been strength in Paul's throw to penetrate the feathers and fat, but the condor managed to thrash and drive the point deeper. Paul and Tynan tried to get closer, but the bird, lying on its back and thrusting with its claws and its beak while shrilly screaming, was too dangerous to approach. The two men had provided sport and proven their courage. A sharpshooter of the Aerie Police finished the condor with a single shot to the skull, and everyone clapped, including Paul and Tynan, who shook hands. It was customary that the winning pike man got as his trophy the severed head, and the clubman the wings; but if the bird had to be shot, the head went to the shooter and the wings were left in the snow for two weeks. Licia had removed her hat and scarf and tossed a kerchief to the two men. Paul and Tynan had looked at each other, and in that moment a controversy had been born. Gallantly, Paul had picked it up after conferring with Robert, and both men had returned it to her. Her name, she said, was Alicia Krings. It was then that Paul recognized the angry older man beside her as Councilman Krings.

Tonight he held his glass, staggering slightly as she stood in his doorway. "Hello."

"Hello," she said. Smartly dressed, with long, slender legs and a fine figure, she was five years younger than Paul. Rumor had it many men had courted her, and Krings had driven them all off, some under threat of their lives. Being on the Council, he could get away with that.

She was lovely and Paul was shocked. She looked at Paul with clear hazel eyes. Then she looked quickly down at her hands and awkwardly twirled her sunglasses, "Won't you ask me in?"

"Of course." He stepped aside.

She walked into his apartment, as was her right under aerie law. "I felt that I must get to know you."

"I am flattered."

She offered the kerchief. "This was meant for you, although the other man also was beautiful."

He bowed slightly, putting it in his pocket. "If you had warned me, I would have worn something more appropriate, and I would have gotten flowers."

"You know what is right," she said.

"I beg you to educate me if I don't."

"May I sleep with you tonight?" The words were ritual.

"My heart beats fast at the thought." The words were from a poem about medieval romance, written during the Middle Ages, and discovered under an altar in France as salvagers brought what they could to trucks for transport to the Swiss Alps. That had been during the melting of the glaciers, but before the comets and volcanoes.

She was beautiful. They stared at each other, and he wondered if she felt the way he did. This was to be no one-night reward for a condor baiting game well brought off. He could see the hunger written in her eyes, and he hoped she was falling in love with him as he was falling in love with her. She seemed strong, yet innocent, and he knew much about her when she said: "My father is very jealous and violent, but you are brave. Maybe you, who kill condors, can take me from my father. Otherwise I will grow old alone. I will have no children and I will walk down the mountain before I am old."

"I don't want to dishonor your father."

She unbuttoned her brown jacket, revealing a fine creamy silk blouse underneath. "I have come and you have accepted me. If you send me away, it will dishonor me, and if you dishonor me, you have dishonored my father. If on the other hand you treat me well, it will honor my father. No matter what I do with a man, it will anger my father, but you will not dishonor him if you keep me with you."

Paul laughed, though all sorts of dreadful implications flickered through his mind. Aerie law was about survival; it was harsh and merciless, and for a moment he pictured himself being sent down the mountain with only food and clothing to keep him alive for a day or two. "You have a sharp mind. If you weren't so beautiful, I would be panicking."

But she was preoccupied with her thoughts and did not hear him. "You see, I have never slept with a man. My father never even allowed me to date during high school or college. And now I have to get away from him. It's not just that you are beautiful and brave." She looked down, biting her lip, and her fingers stopped working the second button of her blouse loose, a heavy round button of the same luxurious material. "You see, I heard that you may be sent to the new world, and I thought you might take me with you. Then I could truly be free."

5. New World—Year 3301

The derelict mother ship with its priceless library burst into flames halfway across the sky. A thick trail of black smoke widened, grew longer. The air shook, and the ground shook. Buffalo herds scattered in flight, running very swiftly close together. The black contrail, twinned with a white one of condensation, roared on across the sky and down over the horizon like an ancient express train on its tracks. Just over the horizon, an explosion slammed through the air.

At least nobody had been aboard the mother ship—assuming the other two lifeboats had successfully detached. But all six pioneers had awakened from their long sleep, rubbing each other, offering comfort for sore limbs and aching backs. The life support systems had functioned beautifully—a tribute to the best minds in all the world's aeries—and the six were intact and robust. The mother ship had inserted itself into orbit—evidently, Paul now knew, too low and too slow—and the lifeboats had auto-launched. Licia had handled her well enough, until—

The alien world returned to its vibrant normal self. Buzzing insects nuzzled and droned. Big colorful flowers bobbed on long red stems. Licia took out the range finder gadget, a black radio which she mounted on Paul's backpack but whose earphones she wore herself, so that a thin cable connected them.

"Hear anything?" he asked, shifting the heavy radio from one side to the other.

She held up a hand. "Tremendous amount of static, that's about it. We'll have to climb to the highest point around. Dammit, the battery is weak."

The alien grass was thick-bladed and scoop-stemmed, and scraped against their boots as Paul and Licia sought the highest ground, a grassy hill about a mile away.

Paul and Licia descended to the plain below in long, easy strides. He was more accustomed to shuffling through snow. "Earth must have been like this once," she said.

6. Old World—Year 2299

Paul was on his way out, but then Krings was on his knees, blubbering, "Menard, for the love of God."

Paul closed his eyes. He had hoped this very moment would never happen. He would rather have faced a wild condor in deadly combat. He would rather have faced Krings in manly combat. But this was a humiliation for both of them. He hoped nobody in the Aerie would ever learn of it.

Krings' eyes were wide with pleading, "Please, she is young and headstrong. She's all I've got. They'll banish me. Oh God, Menard..."

Paul looked out through the thick window. He noted how greenish light lay in the prism of the window's edge. Aerie law was cruel and inexorable. Yes, Krings was finished, and he should be a man about it. Paul thought ahead to the long space voyage. What if the hoped-for planet turned out to be some horror of raging poisonous storms? It took courage to live, no matter what. And yet he could not bring himself to say anything to Krings. He wanted to say: "Stop humiliating us both." Instead he shoved the kneeling man out of his way and walked out. He heard Krings pleading behind him: "Menard, for the love of God! Menard!"

7. New World—Year 3301

At the top of the hill, they caught a faint signal. Licia heard it first. He admired the way the wind blew in her brown hair, the way she raised her nose to the air like a young horse. She was strong, and he was growing hungry for her. But not now. "It's Tynan's," she said handing him the earphones without a flicker of changed emotion.

He listened to the faint beeping sound amid the blizzard of static. It grew stronger as he pointed the gadget. "That way."

Later, at the bottom of the hill, Paul tested the water. It was safe, and they drank deeply. "Good water is half the battle," he said.

She agreed. "SheuXe was right. It's livable." A tear formed in each of her eyes. "It's wonderful that they would have known. That they could send us here knowing that." She sobbed. "We were a pretty wonderful—."

"—Civilization," he said completing her sentence. "Not great enough." Here they had another chance. But she knew that. He did not need to say it. He'd do his own grieving. He knew it came at the oddest moments. He knew that well.

8. Old World—Year 2299

Paul and Gregory had succeeded in landing a trank pellet in the neck of the baby white condor thrashing its ten-foot wings in their trap. Dr. Mannering would pay well for the new research subject. Baby whites were rare.

Gregory, 14, held a coiled rope and waited for his 17-year-old brother to issue directions. Paul saw the sky was clear blue; not a bird in sight. He handed his rifle to Gregory. "You stay here, I'm going back to get help bringing the bird home."

Paul hurried back on the trail through the rugged cliffs with their smooth embankments of snow. The piled domes and cubes of the Aerie shone golden despite their dark towers and bleak walls. A thin powder of ice and snow stung Paul's face, making him squint as he crossed the narrow gangway across the last fissure.

He went with the intention of summoning one or two Aerie cops. As he approached the leeward portal in the high, pitted Aerie wall, he heard a commotion. It was in a separate, low building surmounted by an immense radio dish. He'd nearly forgotten in the excitement of his catch—most of the Aerie leaders would be gathered in the lab, marveling over the transmissions from an intelligent civilization 25 light years away. General Scientist Citizen SheuXe, leader of the Aerie, had only this week announced they had begun receiving the transmissions in Dr. Mannering's lab.

Paul entered the radio lab. First thing he saw was a jumble of winking lights and coiled humming wires. Two dozen or more white-coated scientist citizens stood about drinking hot coffee, listening to what sounded like a mass of loud radio static.

Paul found Dr. Mannering, the chief scientist and director of education. "We found a baby white! I came to get help so we could bring it in. Got caught in one of our—."

Dr. Mannering shook him roughly by the shoulders. "Where is your brother?" White coats crowded all around. Paul's stomach sank and he pointed over his shoulder.

Mannering bellowed: "Guns everybody, snow suits, quick!"

Paul realized he'd made a mistake. He ran out the doorway and back down the trail, out the gate, toward the fissure. Behind him he heard curses and scrambling feet. A siren began to keen. Paul ran across the fissure, wood rocking and pounding under his feet. He ran breathlessly across the snowy plain. The sun hung like a frozen star over the ghostly mountain tops. Paul heard a helicopter cough into life.

For all the help and all the love of God, there was nothing more to be done.

A vast white blanket, flapping slowly, sank down under the cruel spires, smothering two lone and last gun shots. The sun hung ever more cruelly, a red spot in the faraway sky, as the two condors, mother and child, flew away. Their chests were spattered red, and their claws dripped with gore.

9. New World—Year 3301

An outcrop of brown cliffs rose about two miles away, a logical place to go, higher ground. Survive, said a small voice sounding remarkably like SheuXe's in Paul's head; Conquer.

"From high ground, we might be able to spot the other two lifeboats," Licia said as she and Paul rested on a large flat rock. They sipped water and tore open foil packets containing thawed meal bars. "Taste that?" she said, closing her eyes. "Raspberry. My mother used to have a little garden in a sunny spot under the west windows, before she died. She grew things like this and I especially remember the raspberries."

"I never had raspberries," Paul said without rancor; he'd long accepted that she came from a much higher social position and had many more privileges. "Is that the tart, sweet taste?"

She nodded. She interlocked one hand with his.

"I like the bready part, what is it, oats and grains?" He scanned the horizon as he chewed. "We should have seen some smokes by now," he said, wiping his mouth. "All the lifeboats are equipped with signal rockets and smoke generators."

"They would certainly have seen ours," Licia said. "A little unintentional humor there."

"I smell goat shit," Paul said.

She laughed and wrinkled her nose. "Buffalo poop." She pointed. Far off, the buffalo-like creatures that had run in fright had resumed grazing. The air had a pissy, musky oxen smell. Strange, this rich-life planet. The Aerie, by contrast, had had fewer smells, most of them either to do with cleansers or else with mustiness in abandoned corridors. "We can live here, Paul."

"I know," he said, "it's great."

"And scary." She looked around uncomfortably. "It's all so wide open. We don't have to hide from the snow and the cold. You know what scares me most? What scared me to think about even before we left Earth? The idea of sleeping on the ground in the open. I know we have all the gizmos and gadgets, but still—."

He nodded, well understanding. Hiding his own fear, he patted the gun on his belt and then the one on her belt, but she didn't look convinced, and neither was he. "Let's get moving," he said. It seemed like the best thing to do—walking a step ahead of their fears and uncertainties.

They passed several groves of trees, one or two with small animals that nibbled at hanging leaves. Like the buffalo they had spotted earlier, these animals had shaggy, powerful hind legs and small forelegs. These animals had foot-long snouts for pulling down their fodder. When the humans drew near, the animals bolted quickly in a thrashing welter.

"Good runners," Paul said.

"Probably means there are faster predators."

"I'll be you're right."

She kicked a stone. "Six people against a whole world."

"Don't be dramatic."

About an hour after they came to the foot of the cliffs. A reed-choked, swampy area spread under the steep stone face, which was pasty white in color and crumbly. They paused for a few minutes, eyeing the patchy brown water amid the reeds for signs of anything unfriendly. "I guess we do have to keep a look around us at every minute," Licia said.

The sun, N60, had declined visibly in the sky, and there was a cool breeze filled with warm but unfamiliar scents. "We should get up there before dark," he said.

"Right. High ground." She picked her way across grassy and rocky clumps across the swamp, and he followed. "Paul, what about the Senders? We have not found any trace of them yet."

"Yes. Seeing all the ruins wasn't exactly encouraging." In the mother ship, the six pioneers had been able to plan their descent very carefully, even though everything had later gone wrong. They'd expected to find a vibrant but benign space civilization of people much like themselves. The low-density raster images received by Aerie dishes, which themselves were centuries old and no longer optimal, offered only muddy feelings for the aliens' exact appearances.

As they reached dry soil at the foot of the cliffs, darkness came rapidly. Far away, something roared, a sound like a ship's siren, and Licia jumped against him so suddenly he was scared both by the bellowing and by her movement. They stood together, holding each other, and trembling unashamedly. "Paul, let's get to the top of the hill." It was the aerie-borns' instinct to get to high ground. Quickly, they slipped on their heavy work gloves. She followed as he plunged forward. They attacked the dry chalky soil, clinging to a scraggly branch here and a thorny bush there. He could hear thorns ripping at the impervious surfaces of the gloves. Halfway up, reluctantly, he snapped on the small lamps in his collar, and Licia did the same. "Hate to do it. Might give us away, but we have no choice."

"Just a few minutes," she said panting.

"There's the top. Whoa." He hoisted himself around a boulder and emerged on a clearing backset with dense woods.

"Not going in there tonight," Licia said.

"Right. Here, let's set up."

The air was thinner and cooler on the plateau. SheuXe's master plan had provided them with an ideal camp site based on things he'd researched in old army manuals, made of nylon and metal composite struts, and weighing no more than 40 pounds. They began with an alarm perimeter—a thin wire, stretched through the trees in a circle fifty feet in diameter, and grounded to a small body-heat detector. In the center, they erected a tent just big enough for both to lie in. Around that they erected a secondary perimeter consisting of an alarm-rigged shield of dark-camo nylon that blocked the view of their tent. Inside the perimeter, they fired up a small stove that gave off almost no smoke or light, but enough heat to warm up some rations. The stove also gave off a an odor, outside the human range of smell, that was described by the citizen-chemists as "peppery," and which would wipe out any predator's sense of smell for as long as it stayed around, which probably would not be long. They laid their hand guns and rifles in the tent, ready to grab, along with strong flashlights. Without trenches or berms, SheuXe had told his pioneers in class, their only real strategy was to always keep a person on guard while the others slept. If something did spot them despite the visual shield, and didn't mind the pepper smell, then as it crashed through the outer perimeter, alarm noises and lights would go off, scaring it and rousing everyone. Hopefully the person on guard could fill it (or him) full of energy slashes before it could make it into the tent for a dinner of humans. ("What if we are separated?" someone, Nancy Tynan maybe, Paul couldn't remember, had asked in class. SheuXe, diminutive, spectacled, white-haired-balding, forever in a white lab coat, unassuming, yet authoritative and aware of his genius, had shrugged and said in his high, thin voice: "Keep your sense of humor." And everyone had laughed.)

As they ate, the twin moons shone like cracked pennies in a field of stars. Because there was no light pollution from cities, nor industrial pollution—and they'd seen no signs of natural pollutants like volcanoes or forest fires from orbit—the sky was so clear that the stars formed an almost continuous sheet of photoflash yellow along the plane of the Milky Way.

"Look," Licia said. "Orion."

Paul stared in amazement. He had to look closely, for in this rich display, individual groupings of stars were hard to pick out. "You're right. SheuXe told us we might be able to recognize some Earth constellations, though slightly tweaky because of the different angle."

"Twenty-five light years isn't far in the universe, is it?"

"It's eternity if you can't go back."

"We couldn't go back even while we were still there."

He nodded. "It was a dying world." Seeing Orion, and then the Big Dipper, and the rest of the familiar constellations, in various minor degrees of distention, made him think of the lost libraries. "If just one of the other lifeboats makes it, then we have the observations we made before we auto-launched."

Licia gave a small, confident laugh. "We can figure things out for ourselves. Look, if you follow the outer part of the Big Dipper as if you were throwing out the soup in it, you come to that little star there. That's Polaris, Earth's pole star. See the Little Dipper? Of course if this planet has a pole star, it won't likely be Polaris. We should find some reference points, because—."

He reached out and pulled her to him. She laughed and let him. It felt good to feel her lithe young body in his arms, her smooth skin and bony points pressing against him. They made love while the night deepened around them and invisible breezes rustled through the tall, dense trees, Small animals and nesting birds rumored in dank holes.

A while later, each occupied a separate sleeping bag. Paul lay propped on one elbow. Licia lay on her back, eyes half-closed. Fragile moonlight turned the nylon tent gently aglow, painting a restful luxury around her features. The night was full of tiny sounds—insects, birds, all the things he'd imagined you could hear on Earth before the clouds came. Every so often, something huge and terrifying, and thankfully far away, would bellow with an echo that carried for miles.

"Lish."

"Mm?"

"It's so alien—and yet so familiar somehow."

She opened her eyes and held up a leaf with both hands, She touched the leaf wonderingly in several places, "Yes, I think I know what it is. There's more geometry, somehow, I think. The leaves are square or diamond-shaped or ... and the grass is more leafy, sort of furry." The leaf in her hand was feather-shaped, with the spine at one edge. "Maybe it isn't more geometry, but it's all just different enough to be noticeable."

"Generalization," Paul murmured. SheuXe's grand theory had been that, given there are only 92 naturally occurring elements, and given that planets are common in the universe, and given that the same laws apply equally everywhere, and finally given that we have the Senders broadcasting to us, why should there not be myriad Earths?

"We have to find the others," she said. "We must."

"We'll make it." Paul brushed her forehead with his finger to wipe away the worry lines. She wrapped her arms around him and pressed her face into his chest. She mumbled something.

"What, Lish?"

"It's far behind us, Paul. My father. Your brother. The Aeries. All of it. We can start a new life."

He sighed. "Yes, but it's still all up here." He pointed to his head. "It's like yesterday." He could not even say the other things.

"Sleep now," she said softly, drawing him down beside her. "Warm me."

10. Old World—Year 2299

Souspolitis was a short, dark-haired man with a face thought beautiful by many women. Paul, though honored to be invited to the party at Souspolitis' condominium for being one of the six pioneers, had been warned to avoid him. At 45, Souspolitis was 15 years older than Paul. He was one of the few Aerie dwellers who had not grown white-haired in his forties. All his life he had excelled at school, at work, and at play, and for several years now he had been a member of the ruling Council. He had a lazy, cruel sense of humor that stayed just within bounds.

At the party this evening, he made after-dinner conversation with Master Engineer Krings and two other Aerie leaders. Krings, big and tough, had been drinking heavily. What shocked the party was when Krings threw a glassful of whiskey at Souspolitis and stamped away, slamming doors as he left.

Souspolitis, brushing the droplets off his tuxedo, turned coldly, amiably, toward Dr. Mannering, who happened to have been listening, and asked: "Well, Dr. Mannering? Do you share my opinion?"

Mannering looked uncomfortably into his drink. As usual with Souspolitis the discussion cut close to the quick of Aerie sensitivities. Mannering seemed to think for a minute or two.

Meanwhile, the four-piece combo began to play again, drawing some of the spectators softly out of the circle. Laughter rang out. Aerie people knew time was precious. Little time to debate the obvious.

Souspolitis smiled thinly. "Well, Dr. Mannering?" A small crowd remained, anticipating Mannering's reply. Paul couldn't pull himself away. He had to know what Mannering would say.

"Well, Dr. Mannering?"

Mannering was a big man, with huge hands and a red face surrounded by white hair. His normally crisp blue eyes looked pained, "Well, Krings has been moody lately. He can't seem to agree on anything with SheuXe and myself about this interstellar mission we're designing. He seems to want to salvage Earth." He considered some more, staring down as if the answer lay in his drink. Finally he looked up and shrugged. "Yes, I think you are right and Krings is wrong. Earth will never be home to mankind again. We must put our money on the stars, not down here."

Souspolitis shrugged off his small victory, sipping a drink. The crowd began to drift apart and the music and laughter picked up. So the mission would go forward, Paul thought walking away. At this point, Krings must feel the disapproval of his EarthTwo project was the final nail in his coffin. Paul grew sweaty under the collar, thinking any day now he and Licia would have to confront Krings about their affair.

11. New World—Year 3301

Was it in dreams that beasts roared in the night?

The detector had not gone off yet when Paul and Alicia woke in the cold gray dawn.

They were situated on a bluff overlooking the plains they'd crossed yesterday. The top of the bluff was an unusual composition, of chalky stone set here and there with soil-filled depressions from which vegetation grew. Whatever lived in the dark, impenetrable forest beyond, nothing had come out to eat them, at least during their first night. Paul remembered the Rocky Mountains, however, and took the view that nature was a great fooler.

Paul sat by the campsite cranking a hand-turned heater designed by SheuXe. A prepackaged breakfast was heating up in the core. It was like a good-bye kiss, Paul thought, like a packed lunch from mom and dad for the first school day. Bless the long dead. Soon it would be a matter of what the hunt could bag. He'd been trained to kill condors for sport, initially because his parents thought it was a good society thing, and after Gregory's death he had a personal gripe with the enemy birds.

Nearby, Licia bathed nude in a group of depressions that were filled with rain water rather than soil. She squealed at the cold, and he privately thought he'd rather wait until the noon heat. He longed for one of the old Aerie hot tubs. But it was fun to watch. Her white body was slim, though just rich enough in the thighs and buttocks so she was not skinny. She soaped her round breasts so the dark nipples peeked through foam. Her light-brown hair was plastered wetly around her finely shaped skull. Totally immersing herself to rinse off the soap, she sprang out squealing and wrapped herself in her towel. He wrapped his arms around her for warmth. "You feel like some kind of fish," he said as she made a hard shivering ball of bony shoulders and shoulder blades and stabbing elbows. He dried her bottom while she dried her upper half, and then quick, she climbed back into her suit. "Washing can wait," she declared.

"For a warm, sunny day," he agreed.

"Oh look, Paul," she said a while later. She had discovered a tell-tale ecological anecdote. Beyond a massive, fallen tree trunk was a smaller, different wear pattern in the chalky stone. The pattern was a spattering of small indentations, each an inch or so across, now mossy and glistening with water. Standing for centuries, the tree had dripped rainwater, wearing down the rock in a drizzle from its leaves. Things are the same everywhere, Paul thought. Generalized.

A while later, they sat on the rocky ledge and surveyed the plains through binoculars. Their eyes roved in a panoramic sweep over the land that sank a mile away as much as three hundred feet below. It was an eerie, oppressive landscape with skips of wind-chased fog.

"I hear something," Paul said tersely. "Something's going to happen."

"There," Licia said, "just coming out of the marshes under the cliffs."

Paul saw them a second after she did. At first they seemed like just another innocuous element in a puzzling vista—small dog-like animals that bounded randomly through tall grass. They were tan, with short snouts. Paul studied them through his binocs. He noted sharp teeth, black savage eyes. Some distance away against the wind, buffalo grazed in somnolence, up to their bellies in mist. Most animals here seemed to have small forelimbs and heavy hind legs. It suggested running, which suggested predation. For some reason, Paul remembered SheuXe's words again: Survive, Conquer. Men had not come to N60A to be servants of the Senders. They had come either to coexist or to conquer. No other end could justify the long journey. SheuXe had made these things unarguably clear.

The lead dog crouched in the grass, sniffing the air.

High up, several birds floated silently, waiting. From habit, Paul worried more about them than about the dogs. The dogs moved through the grass in stealthy, purposeful formation, toward a cluster of nibbling, unsuspecting buffalo.

Paul and Licia exchanged understanding looks. They watched with eager fascination as the dogs took their time. A moment later, the contest between dogs and buffalo began. The lead dog, having picked out a target, blended back into the pack. Now, from either end of the formation, two dogs darted forward out of cover to harass the buffalo. The larger animals, kicking so their powerful hind limbs sprayed soil, ran in a fanning pattern. Now Paul understood the reason for the dogs' flanking maneuver. The marked buffalo ran twice as quickly as the fastest dog.

Paul glanced over and saw that Licia was glued to her binocs. Her expression was aloof, but her cheeks glowed pink with concentration. The four dogs ran hard, coming in on the buffalo from both sides. Anticipating where the animal's trajectory would take it, they hit like darts. One dog missed and landed rolling. Another dog was caught in the whirlwind grinder of the buffalo's legs; the broken dog was lost in the grass. This caused the marked animal to stumble while its fellows got away. It fell down, and tried to rise, but the clinging dogs attacked its two short forelegs. Tendons torn up, forelegs useless, the animal's eyes grew large and it showed its teeth in a terrified grimace even as it lay down to die. In seconds, the rest of the dog pack arrived, swarming, to dissect the carcass. High up, the gliding birds waited their turn.

"Fascinating," Licia said. She hadn't taken her binocs off the contest.

Paul smiled. "We just learned the ropes, kid."

"Nothing really new there, Paul."

"That's what I mean. We know how to play these games. We'll do okay here."

"Don't be too cocky."

"I'm a young man, full of testosterone. I'm supposed to be cocky."

"Have a brain, darling. You'll find it refreshing." She could be so cool, this Krings woman who put on airs. She stayed glued to the binocs. Her frosty elegance succumbed to a faintly passionate, almost voyeurish breathlessness.

In minutes, the dogs were done, carrying off bits of offal and bone, leaving a bloody carcass that would provide hours of feeding. Already, birds—avians, dreaded from Aerie memory—roosted on the scarlet rack. "We could stay a day or two and see the whole food chain come out," Licia said.

He slid across to her and gently pushed the binocs down. "Brains, my bloody arse. I spoused you, didn't I? I took you away from that old pedophile, incontinent, impotent wash-up you were spoused to against your will. Did he ever try to come in your bed at night?"

She rolled over on her back and gripped the chest of his jumpsuit with both fists. "He wouldn't have dared. I would have killed him."

"That's what I like to hear, that I spoused something worthwhile. Show me what you've got."

Never taking her glazed eyes off his, she pulled apart her front, then pulled up her quilted undershirt. He felt wild with hunger, seeing her smooth skin, stomach held flat by gravity, belly button a squiggle in soft flesh, nipples half exposed under the light quilting material which would go no higher. He noticed she had put red lacquer on her fingernails, and their color, and her intention, drove him further. "Show me. Show me."

She opened her front all the way down, showing him. Pushing her panties down with one hand buried in walnut-colored pubic hair, she gripped him around the back of the neck. "You took me from him, didn't you? You stood up against him when no other man had the courage." She pulled his head close to hers. He held back, just to wind her up more. She raised her head to take hungry snatches at his mouth, licking him. Then he could only make the final leap, getting into her, slamming repeatedly against her good full softness until he reared up, roaring, and spurted into her. Spurted into her, into space, into time, into lost Earth, into the glory that they had gotten here and were alive, spurted into the very soil of this place that a million descendants might spring up from the ground. She writhed under him, wailing again and again "yes!" between deep intakes of breath each time he slammed against her.

Afterward, they lay together breathless and sated. He had his eyes closed, still seeing various shimmering earth colors. "That was great," he heard her say as she kissed his hand. It was all the energy she had left.

"This planet must be some sort of stimulant," he said. "Or it's the fresh air. The sight of blood. The thought that we made it this far. The endless possibilities."

She rolled on top of him and touched his nose. "It's an aphrodisiac and we're going to do lots of those from now on."

As they packed their gear, ready to look for Robert and Nancy Tynan, Paul saw something in the distance. He lifted his binoculars for a look. "Lish, look past the buffalo's body. To the right, what do you see?"

She looked through her binoculars. Timid sunshine began to drive mist away. The sky was turning warm and blue. She studied the plains. "There is a line of some kind, a road? A road, Paul, it is a road! My God! A road!"

"The Senders were here," he said. "Intelligent life. Let's go down and have a look. Keep your rifle handy, because this may change everything."

"I was just beginning to enjoy you and I being Adam and Eve."

12. Old World—Year 2299

The radar man waved from his plexi bubble atop the Aerie's highest tower: "All clear, no avians." His voice crackled over the speakers. The sun glared on the bubble's silvery top.

Paul stood not far from Licia on one of the lower escarpments with a crowd of other onlookers. Licia stood by her father, Citizen Engineer Krings. This little experiment was his defining statement. He had bet the store that the surface of the Earth was becoming more livable. Paul felt torn between the hope that Krings might be right, so he'd be less cantankerous, and the hope that Krings were wrong, because otherwise the star flight project to N60A would be canceled. The radar dish rotated evenly on its axis. On the ramparts high up stood dark-silhouetted riflemen, their weapons ready should any avians threaten the onlookers.

The center of attention was a ten-foot yellow drone with long, narrow wings, sitting on a wooden runway aimed away from the Aerie. The plane was to penetrate the black clouds below and send back television pictures in video and infra-red. It was to be man's first look at Earth's surface in generations.

A technician began reading off breathability soundings on a scale Krings had devised. "Index, one oh," the tech singsonged over the loudspeaker. The "1.0" was the index in fresh air at Aerie level. "One oh, one oh," he repeated.

Loud as gunfire, the unmuffled engine fired up, shooting kerosene in black blobs.

"One oh, allowing for fuel porting."

With a jerk, the plane cut loose and its little rubber wheels whirled down the long ramp. Paul and the others watched, fascinated, as it described a long beautiful curve through free air. It rose up slightly.

"One oh, steady."

Quickly growing small and distant, it curved in a lazy circle while Paul wanted to hold his breath. Finally it eased down into the lightning-studded clouds.

"Point nine. Point eight. Point seven. Point six. Point five."

Paul and the others crowded around a series of monitoring screens. Dr. Mannering in his billowing white lab coat stood near the engineering console watching a flickering stream of numerical information on backlit readouts.

"Point five. Critical line." If it dropped below fifty per cent, Paul knew, Krings would be wrong. He'd predicted an average of point six, up from point five where the soundings had held steady for the past twenty years.

Sound pickups on the plane generated a blast of engine noise and whistling wind as the craft penetrated two miles of deadly cloud cover.

"Point five."

A loud whistling noise signaled the beginning of the engine's suffocation from lack of oxygen. The technicians switched off their flight control monitors. The plane was now in free glide. Already, the technicians exchanged triumphant handshakes. The mood, however, was muted, for there was nothing more to celebrate than the technical accomplishment of a toy-like plane flight.

"Point four." A murmur of disappointment ran through the crowd. "Point three." Krings looked shocked. "Point two five. Point two five. Steady. Point two three." Disbelief, rage, defeat, denial, tragedy spread across Krings's features. The air was no longer breathable at all to humans at the surface. The Earth they'd known, that their race and most related life had evolved on, was virtually dead. And the clouds were rising at several feet per year.

The plane's cameras now used battery power to send back a series of grayscale stills that were threaded like jerky movie footage. The crowd became silent in the Aerie.

"Point two two. Steady. Point two three. Point two two."

For a long time, the picture was a uniform, cloudy gray. The technician no longer bothered to read the soundings as they dropped into meaninglessness.

Rocky outcroppings cast sharp outlines as the plane dropped to within two hundred feet of the surface.

Somebody gasped.

The plane quivered and prepared to break up in the air if it did not crash first as it entered the lowermost, thickest layer of sulfurous gases.

A murmur of comment arose.

Paul saw a huge shape moving around. Someone screamed. The scream was quickly muffled by the horror of realization.

A gasp of revulsion arose from the spectators.

Two immense, humped bodies writhed in combat. Other viperous shapes, surmounted by serpentine necks, looked this way and that, searching for whatever unholy prey became these inheritors of the poisoned earth.

Last, before the cameras abruptly ceased to transmit, they recorded a writhing mass: An entire herd of the abominations.

"You see," Paul heard Souspolitis say to Krings, "there is no going back."

Paul looked through the crowd, and felt saddened by Krings's crushed look, Souspolitis' predatory glint of triumph, and Licia's pathetic attempts to console her father.

13. New World—Year 3301

Rifles ready, Paul and Licia walked along the ancient roadway in the general direction of the Tynan signal. The road was of L-shaped stones that stretched interminably in either direction. The surface was remarkably flat, and the stones were so tightly linked and joined that almost no grass grew between them. However, grass grew high along the sides, perhaps because of moisture trapped under the stones. Here and there were spoon-sized natural depressions in the road surface; these had filled with soil, and now harbored greenish-blue clumps of moss. A hopelessness sighed out of the silence—of trying to recapture something lost forever. The Senders? Those enigmatic beings who had signaled to Earth that it was safe for carbon-based life to come, to revel in a culture spanning the stars? A strange lethargy came over Paul and Licia as they slowly walked mile after mile. They had little to say to each other. Wind keened softly over mute stones. Grass and bushes grew out of moist cracks in the roadway. They stopped once to check their rifles and make sure their sidearms were loaded and ready for combat.

Conquest, Paul thought. "A thousand years ago, there may have been civilization here. Today, it's just cracks and dust. What is left to conquer?"

"Huh?"

"Just thinking out loud."

"Save your optimism." She added with a less haughty look, glancing around: "Feels haunted."

Paul felt a chill despite the warm wind, as if they were in a giant graveyard. The large flat stones felt soft and mossy under their feet. They walked cautiously and kept their rifles ready. Paul remembered the wind being like this on a gentle sunny day, long ago, when they'd laid Gregory to rest. That was in the cemetery along the western wall, where the sun tended to keep the snow clear, and much of the year there was a grassy stretch from end to end of the Aerie. But this world seemed tranquil. The eight foot wide road, marked in places as if by wheel ruts, seemed haunted by dead voices. When they'd laid his parents to rest a year or two later, they'd had to dig through three meters of snow and then thaw the ground. Paul had walked away when the thawing began, unable to face what lay in the ground.

Here and there, they noticed new details. Some broad-leafed plants. A patch of red round berries. A pair of triangular-bodied, ten-legged spiders wove a foamy net between themselves across a number of bamboo-like baby tree trunks. Licia pointed to a field of pink flowers packed in a carpet not far away by the roadside. That reminded Paul of the millions of plant seeds from Earth, lost with the lifeboat and the mother ship. He bent to examine some wheat-like plants.

Licia stopped and wiped her forehead. "It's good to be in the sun. We could never do this on Earth." At that moment, they heard a scream. Paul whirled and aimed his rifle, ready to spray a stream of deadly needles. Nothing. They stood in place, turning warily.

"Some animal," she said.

"More like a woman. Or a child."

"Sounded scared." She added: "Too high pitched for Robert or Nancy."

Then they heard yapping. "Dogs again," Paul said. They listened intently. A small bird shot by overhead. Insects chirruped.

A dog screamed. Then, a different sound: of a human being in mortal fear. Licia's face paled. "Ghosts," she whispered.

Paul heard more sounds from a depression hidden in high grass and reeds by the roadside. He wanted to investigate, but he wanted her close behind for her protection more than his. "Quick, that way."

They crashed through a mass of swampy reeds, their boots sucking in mud. Another shrill scream of mixed fear and pain sounded. Furious thrashing added to the noise of their own passage through the reeds. Paul felt fear, but he also felt the old condor-hating blood fury. If fight he must, then fight he would.

Before he could react, there was a ripping sound in the reeds. Lightning quick on powerful hind legs, dogs flashed past exposing their teeth and melded away on either side. Paul and Licia stopped short in a clearing among reeds.

No more dogs.

"God," Licia said.

In the clearing were two blue boys.

"Don't be afraid," Paul said to them, to Licia, to himself.

Aliens.

Or are we?

A last limping dog slithered away through the brush. Paul hung the rifle over his shoulder. Licia did the same with hers. They stood face to face with the aliens.

Boys, Paul thought, two of them. Young men. Actually, their skin was a dark clay color, brown, verging into dull blue. It was smooth except for splotches of bright red blood. They looked very scared and very human. Their faces were squarish, with slitty eyes, and they could almost have passed as some exotic cross-breed of all the races of Earth, except that their figures had an elongated something about them, something foreign, something just barely or not quite strange. And each had a mane of lion-colored, tawny hair down his spine.

Here, now, at this moment, on this lush world, were youths, children!

And where these were, there were undoubtedly more. Paul found it hard to place their similarity or dissimilarity with Aerie people.

After all, by the 2200's, there were no distinct racial groupings anymore. Earth's surviving million had been a hodge-podge of all possible phenotypes.

The six pioneers had brought to N60A most of the gene pool of their race.

In the long term, the moon would not pan out as a replacement for the lost paradise of Earth.

The planets had been too far to reach en masse and impossible to terraform with resources on hand.

Many aerie people had quietly and voluntarily ceased having children, knowing there was no hope; few wanted their beloved offspring to face the grim last generations.

The human race had begun committing a bleak though dignified suicide.

The two boys held their weapons close as they stared at their liberators.

"Look," Licia said, pointing. Both boys were tied to the ground by a single heavy cord around one ankle, looped in the middle through a stone ring in the ground.

"It's some kind of test," Paul guessed, stepping forward. He ducked back as the boys brandished huge spears. Several mangled dog bodies strewn about attested to the savagery of the combat Paul and Licia had interrupted.

The boys kept their weapons aimed toward Paul and Licia and stared with large, glazed eyes. Then one of the boys folded, dropping to the ground. Loss of blood, Paul thought. Licia took out her first-aid kit.

14. Old World—Year 2299

Paul, 19, had reached the point of truth in his test aerie. This was the seventh and last night he'd have to spend in this hell. If he could only hold out until dawn! The night was black and scratched full of stars. Paul huddled in his concrete shell which was barely large enough to hold him. The cold seemed to eat him alive. He must stay awake. Must stay awake,—and his mind swam through one delirium after another.

No moon.

This was the Aerie's way of teaching a young man about himself, about itself, about the universe. It cured the youthful urge to wander. It was childhood's destroyer if nothing else had been. For Paul, his childhood lay buried with Gregory. He did not have to be here. If you hoped ever to be a member of the ruling elite, or better yet the Council, this was one of the trials you had to undergo.

The soft part of Paul longed to be back in the Aerie. Oh the soft warm girls in the Aerie. The Aerie was all-providing. Never, never, he vowed, would he violate Aerie law.

The hard part of Paul cursed those comforts. He trembled with delirium. If he could only hold out until dawn. He'd had only melted ice to drink. Nothing to eat for days. He'd killed and eaten a baby bird. Killed it with a stick he'd found. No heat, no fire. He'd pawed grunting desperately over it. Its blood had been warm as he'd sucked on its still-beating heart after piercing its chest with the stick. That was days ago.

Ice, everywhere, ages old. The world was a museum of stalactites. Of shifting silhouettes. Sometimes, when he was half out of his mind, it seemed the Aerie was abandoned, its windows gone, the ice inside like a cancer. Then he felt more alone than ever, the last man in the universe.

Not far away was a box containing a radio transmitter. All he'd have to do was push the button and the rescue team would come. One heard stories of young men trying to claw their way aboard the helicopter in a change of mind, too late, and being kicked and punched back into the snow. Some boys lasted the full seven days, but most didn't. It was no great shame to push the button after the third or fourth day. Some had been found frozen to death. Those who'd terminated early had gladly, with relief, though with a little lasting regret, consigned themselves to the role of ordinary resident rather than Citizen. Paul had decided against that. It was success or death. Those were the only two choices he allowed himself.

His world had narrowed to a few dozen yards of frozen horror. Mostly he dreamed, whether he was awake or asleep. After a while waking and sleeping became the same things. He couldn't walk anymore. His hands were blue, and soon he couldn't bear to look at them.

Was that dawn sweeping a white sheet over the snow or was it—?

From here on, he must stay on his feet, for if he lay down he'd fall asleep and drift into the cold mouth of death.

No, the sheet of dawn was like a pink wine, sparkling with splashes of gold.

It was still night out; the glare was simply his pain.

He gritted his teeth and damned all eternity, all night. He would fight for the day, or die, and be welcome doing it, wind up beside Gregory.

As they told him later, they'd found him standing in the hut covered with ice. At first they were sure he'd frozen to death standing up, his features distorted with runneling ice, an eerie figure leaning against the wall, frozen to it, leaning on a stick. In fact, as they lowered him into the stretcher, they weren't sure it was he— one nurse thought it was a legendary old man of the mountain who'd replaced Paul.

15. New World—Year 3301

Licia pressed the initiative with a roll of gauze. Soon the spears went down on one side, the rifle on the other. Licia and the boy bent over the prostrate youth. The boys spoke in a flowing language rich with syllables.

"Wonder where their people are?" Paul said

Licia hefted a gauze roll from one hand to the other, "Well, they talk, so maybe we can learn the lingo. Remember, we are the aliens here."

"God, but they're like us, aren't they?"

Licia nodded, busily applying her dressings. "Got to get them home, wherever that is. They need more care than we can provide."

"I'd be afraid to give them anything of our medicines," Paul said.

"Hello there," Licia said firmly, tying a knot in a bandage. "Licia." She pointed to herself. "Licia," she repeated.

Both boys looked at her with intelligent eyes. Licia repeated her name. Then she pointed to Paul and said "Paul."

Paul pointed to himself and said: "Paul."

The two boys labored to say: "Li-sha, Po-wul." Then they burst into self-conscious smiles, as earthly children might. Paul and Licia exchanged looks. He'd never seen her look quite so independent and accomplished and pleased.

"Your name?" Licia asked.

The two young men who stood before them in clay-blue pendulous nakedness were out of breath and exhausted. They appeared grateful at having been rescued. "Amda," the taller and more slender of the two introduced himself. He pointed to his companion and said: "Dunda." Dunda offered a chubby, complacent grin.

"They're sweet," Licia said.

Conquer, the voice inside Paul said suddenly, so surprisingly he felt flustered for a moment, thinking he'd spoken out loud. He suppressed the despair bordering on panic that arose in him. It was maddening to think that they had to share this world and therefore be dependent on the good or ill wishes of unknown people. To think that they had come all this way, perhaps to be wiped out like gnats by some disease, or a random arrow, or a bit of poison food. Then again, every kilometer along the thousand year journey had involved life and death risk. He posited the conditional: trust, but verify.

"Paul?"

He relaxed. "All right. We'll go with them. But keep your eyes open. Ask them if they know anything of the Tynans."

16. New World—Year 3301

Home turned out to be a sunken village amid a sea of waving wheat. Licia worked hard to interpret, to learn the language as they walked—Paul had little patience for it—but no, the boys knew nothing of an object that flew from the air and crashed into the ground. The day grew warm, and they stripped off their flight suits, leaving thin olive drab fatigues. At times, Paul felt overwhelmed by the strangeness of their new world, especially of finding human-like beings who walked and spoke and could quickly learn to understand universal gestures made with the hands and head. There must be some deeper mystery to how life had spread in the neighborhood of Old Earth. But there were too many more immediate and pressing problems—finding the Tynans and the Wengs; finding a place to set up a human village.

After several hours on the post road with Amda and Dunda, making good progress despite sprains, cuts, and bandages, they came to a settled area. The smells of smoke and cooking told Paul that. He spotted distant shapes running toward the village—no doubt bringing news of visitors.

As they drew near the village, a wall of high reeds grew up on either side of the road. Evidence, Paul thought, that the settlement had a plentiful supply of water. He heard excited whispering in the reeds. Occasionally a shadowy face peered out. A dark hand would push aside the reeds, opening a spy hole; and just as quickly it would close.

The knot of emotional men waiting for them in the village was another matter. The road dipped down into a bowl-shaped depression containing about twenty mud-brick houses. The houses stood around a central plaza of hard-beaten dirt with a large kiln just off center. The post road continued through the village and over the horizon. The hillsides all around had neatly planted gardens.

About a half dozen compact, powerful men blocked the way. They wore long leather loin cloths and armless leather vests. Paul stared at them in apprehension, not for the odd assortment of weapons they sported—wood staff, dully menacing machete—but to spot any really alien traits of physiognomy that would make shivers run up and down his spine. Licia seemed to have the same thought, for she said: "You know, if they'd just kill us right now, that would be good human behavior. But if they turn out to have lots of eyes—." She made a face.

Paul raised his hand in greeting, keeping the other hand on the rifle. Licia did the same. A staccato conversation began between the slender boy and one of the older men present. This man had gray, almost transparent hair, and he was the only one who wore any sort of ornament. On his chest, suspended by a leather thong, was a burnished disk of copper about three inches in diameter. The disk hung with a kind of somber majesty that suited his aura. A staccato conversation ensued between him and the boys. This chief, if that he was, raised his arms in circles, the first contracting downward, the second spreading outward; he made a noise signifying explosion. Paul wondered if they'd actually seen the lifeboat descending. Amda shrugged and appeared to say that they'd been busy tied down and killing dogs, and so had not had the time or the occasion to look about for crashed lifeboats. He pointed constantly back to where he had met the two aliens. During this, the other men waved their weapons with muscular arms and offered vehement advice.

"If we have to shoot our way out," Paul said quietly without looking at his spouse, "I'm going to kill the guy with the disk first. You spray the ones on the right, and I'll take the ones to the left of Mr. Disk."

"Right."

Hearing the click of her safety, he quickly added: "Let's try to avoid it if at all possible."

After a minute or two, the chief raised his arms. Evidently, the boys had convinced him to be grateful for saving them. The chief pointed to himself and said: "Ongka." He had dark, piercing eyes that looked deeply into Paul's soul and made him shiver. The warriors opened an alley of safe passage. Paul and Licia seemed welcome, but with some reserve.

The women and children of the community poured out to stare at their alien guests, to touch their clothing, to laugh nervously to one another and then stare at Paul and Licia.

Paul noticed a side event. Through the whirl of faces, he spotted Ongka further down the village, conferring with two other old men. Several younger men joined them. Ongka turned to the younger men and raised his hand. He issued a series of statements to them; then he waved them off, and they began running in various directions. Odd, Paul thought; were they running to notify others? Maybe it made sense—some warning probably. He shoved the thought aside and returned his attention to the throng around him.

Licia said: "Their women and children, how beautiful. Elongated and graceful." The women all wore cloth skirts. Some wore jacket-like tops, others just a kind of sling bra knotted over one shoulder. The younger women were mostly tall and graceful. Many had faces Paul found attractive, though he could not associate them with one race or another that he'd known on earth, nor could he spot individual details that one could peg—high cheekbones, for example; oriental-style eyes; in fact, they seemed to be more like the Aerie people in that they were all different. Some were lighter, some darker, though all shared that bluish tinge. Their eyes were a source of noticeable beauty. A few had blue or green eyes, though most had brown. A few of the browns were so light their eyes gleamed like maple syrup in the sun, others had eyes dark as forest honey.

Their hair drew his attention, and he tried to sort out the hair-rules in their variety. All the men had manes down the spine like Amda and Dunda. Some, however, also hair atop their heads like Mohawks. Some of the Mohawks grew naturally from ear to ear over the top of the head, while others ran from the forehead to the back of the head. Most of the men had darker, rougher third manes over their shoulders. The women had only light manes down their spines. Many of the women had fine silvery hair atop their heads, almost like Earthly Afro hair, but thinner and finer so one could see through it the dark gleaming curves of the scalp. They smiled and otherwise made facial expressions Paul could understand.

She returned his look directly. "It won't be us." She added: "We're going to have children here, Paul. I don't want my children to suffer."

She had a point there, he had to admit.

The central kiln was about fifteen feet high and roughly circular, with a ten foot diameter. Paul supposed it was a hearth fire that never went out. It had dozens of daubed-mud cubbyholes for baking, roasting, and broiling. "A community stove," Licia said.

"They are a commune," Paul said with a sense of revelation. "Wow, I didn't even learn that in Anthro. But it makes sense."

"You can learn a lot about people from their eating habits," Licia said completing his thought.

An elderly woman knelt before the kiln and extracted a baked something, fowl from a peek through the leaves in which it was wrapped to give it flavor. She offered one to each of them. Feeling ceremonial, Paul accepted with a great show of thanks. Licia muttered: "You're scoring points every minute."

He tasted it. "Mmm..." It was delicious, like baked chicken in sweet, smoky, peppery sauce. Young boys and girls wandered among the crowd, offering side dishes. A few of the side dishes were spicy and smelly beyond tolerance, but one or two resembled baked terrestrial potatoes.

The chief sat on the ground with crossed legs. Beside him sat a dignified elderly woman; his spouse, Paul assumed. Or did they marry here? A young girl with budding breasts brought clay cups and a stone jug. The chief handed a cup to Paul and another to Licia, then drank deeply himself. Paul gingerly tasted a greenish liquid that was cool as if it had come from some deep well. Tiny plant debris floated in the bottom of the jug; it had a refreshing, faintly anise taste.

"We look for our friends," Paul told the alien chief. "Friends landed in sky ships." Licia tried to help tell about it. Ongka nodded sagely, though his thoughts appeared to be elsewhere, and in any case it was doubtful he understood Aerie Anglomex.

The high blue sky was fresh and clean. Paul felt a comforting sense of being surrounded by the village—by its gardens, its homes, its greenery, its birds and insects. Here was a sense of loving and belonging he had never felt before, even in the tightly knit Aerie. Suddenly he caught himself—in the balmy influence of this place, his sense of mission was being diluted, and he realized too late that the drink was acting upon him.

Oh but how it was hitting him. He cursed Ongka, the planet, his own stupidity for walking into this trap. Where the hell was Licia? He couldn't see her anywhere. He couldn't see properly, just blurs all around. He felt paralyzed, as Ongka stared into his eyes. He felt the chief's authority. The disk on Ongka's chest flashed hypnotically in sunlight. Each flash caused Paul to feel a stab through his brain, but the stabs left no pain. Ongka kept flashing the disk into Paul's face. Somehow that disk was important, but Paul didn't know how or why. He felt sleepy and relaxed. The cup fell out of his hand. What a peaceful place this was!

The sun in his face relaxed him. The chief's face—wow, dress him in a tuxedo, send him to one of Souspolitis' parties. What a lustrous intelligence, what a tranquil wisdom radiating from those eyes. Paul began to understand as Ongka's thought-spoke into his mind. Not chief but medicus. Charge of mind and body. Not chief, only medicus. Only Ongka. Ongka's eyes went deeply into Paul's soul. There were eyes Paul never knew he had, and they met Ongka's. Paul felt as if he were swimming inside himself. He was aware of himself in a half-sickly way. He was aware of his guilts and faults, aware of his good and bad qualities. The word "conquest" cringed within him like an insect impaled by the light shooting from Ongka's eyes. Ongka saw it all, his conversations long ago with SheuXe (but could he understand?), the frantic running to save Gregory, Krings crying and blubbering at Paul's feet, all of it. And eyes they were, of fire. The orb of the medicus' skull contained knowledge reserved to himself and those of his profession. The medicine man peered through his soul while Paul could only dimly penetrate the wall of resistance inside the other's mind. Ongka peered deeply into Paul's innermost being. Paul felt the depth of that stare—and realized that, mercifully, Ongka was only looking, not hurting. What power! At the same time, Paul perceived a flotsam of filtered impressions at the edge of the other's mind: only what Ongka would let him see. Paul saw many people crying. He saw a memory of plague and smelled the stench of the dead. Then he saw a vision that conveyed Ongka's profound, sacred excitement: a magnificent city raising its ramps and towers to the sky. In that city rested the soul of everything that he was going to discover on N60A. In that city were the answers to everything mankind had sought in this new world and perhaps on its own.

Somehow, in Ongka's mind, Paul saw an intricate mechanism of copper or bronze, a machine in which moved levers and wheels of mechanistic regularity, layered behind the medicus' face, which still stared deeply into Paul's soul. As darkness reached out of the earth with long fingers and pulled Paul down, he thought helplessly: how strange, this all from a man wearing a loincloth and living in a mud hut.

It was dark out when Paul woke. A dry cool wind stirred among the village huts. This was it. The alien reality. Tallows glowed in a few doorways. Paul sat stiffly upright, feeling chilled and empty.

A baby cried nearby. A cat creature slunk around the stone shelves of the kiln; its eyes glowing like red coals. A woman murmured nearby.

Paul sat up with a terrible start as a door flap was pushed aside. Ongka's copper disk glinted powerfully in the starlight, and behind it glowered the medicus' shadow. Paul stared respectfully; the old man had his attention. An old woman approached bearing a woolen blanket and a steaming cup. Paul felt empty and helpless. He allowed the blanket to be wrapped around him. He drank deeply of a hot, bitter drink. While he drank, he shivered, and hot liquid spilled onto his legs.

Two men lifted him. They carried him through the village. Halfway there his bowels loosed and his legs warmed with it, and he sobbed in humiliation. People cleaned him up. They brought him to a hut where he promptly went back to sleep.

While he slept he dreamed that he was down by a stream in a deep wood. The very air seemed almost the color of moss, like a liquid in a bottle, so deep was he, and sunlight where it got through lay thick like butter. A native girl on a white mare rode by. (Did they know of horses here? even dreaming he was puzzled) She held open her emerald cloak, revealing smooth young skin the color of ripe plums. She had small breasts with brown nipples but he could not make out her hair. Something light, like ice or ivory. Her eyes were slitty, oriental, mysterious. Her waist was narrow and high-set, her pretty navel concave. Her belly and hips widened downward to her legs spread over the horse. A translucent corona of hairs brightened the Y-shape between her thighs. As she rode on, turning her back toward him, she closed her emerald cloak and cast a fading resentful puzzling look at him. For a moment she was Licia. Then again she was not.

Paul awakened when several small children ran laughing and playing into the hut. He sat up with a start. Licia! The rifles! Too late, he realized. Ongka was in control. The children froze and eyed him with childlike frankness. Then they burst into laughter and ran back outside. Paul lay back. His head felt fuzzy. He must have slept for a very long time. He felt safe and relaxed, and certainly sheepish. Ongka had disarmed him as surely as if he'd defeated him in martial arts, throwing him before he'd known what happened. For a moment, he had the illusion of being back on Earth. But it was only a momentary thing. Everything was different here in myriad subtle ways.

A shaft of sunlight poured through a doorway of the adobe hut, striking a pile of sealed stone jars in a corner. Their rifles and packs were neatly—by Licia's hand?—piled in another corner. Where was Licia? He checked the guns. Everything was in fine working order. Nothing was missing, not even the long knives that the natives surely must covet.

He stepped outside. Children shouted as they played hide-and-go-seek around sunken stone slabs. The kiln smoked from dozens of apertures. Women stoked the kiln and prepared leaf-wrapped food for baking. An old woman gave Paul a piece of dry, gamey fowl, which he ate hungrily. In the distance, he saw a smiling Licia, looking neat and rested, holding a baby while several young girls crowded around admiringly. Something disturbed Paul. Conquest. Their thousand year journey must not end by their assimilation into a primitive alien culture.

He started to walk toward her, but Ongka unexpectedly appeared with two elderly men. The medicus smiled disarmingly and touched Paul's shoulder. They sat down together. Children brought steaming tea in stone cups. Ongka traded cups with Paul as a gesture of trust.

They fell into a frustrating conversation in sign language. Ongka shook his hands in the air and made explosion noises. He pointed to the sky and then to the ground. Paul nodded (yes, the mother ship). How many, Ongka wanted to know. Six, Paul indicated in the dust at their feet. He attempted to show that they had landed in three pairs, scattered who knew where. Surprised, he saw that the three men exchanged understanding looks. Could they understand a map? He drew in the dust, adding detail indicating the post road, the mountain plateau. Ongka and his companions, with animated debate, filled in local details. Paul leaned forward and carefully sketched in a rendition of the alien city observed from space. For him, the city was the key. He could not rest until he stood in that place and saw it for himself.

Ongka fixed a long, speculative look upon Paul. Then, using a sharp stick, he carefully sketched circles in the dirt. Central to the circles, he placed a large round stone. On each circle he placed one small stone. Paul felt a shiver crawl around his guts. Ongka placed two tiny chips of stone around one of the small stones. Paul gaped at Ongka. It had taken Earth's finest minds thousands of years to figure out the type of facts this primitive man had casually drawn in the sand. Paul drew a sketch of the planet as he had surveyed it from space. He drew the two large land masses that were its continents and placed a pebble where he thought the village to be. "Akha," Ongka said.

The old men jabbered with delight. They placed stones here and there, naming the villages they knew. There was a comforting, if monotonous, predictability about their language. All villages were something plus ka. So, Ongka's village was Aka, pronounced "Ah-kah."

Paul placed a larger stone where the mysterious city was, perhaps 300 miles due west. Then he held his breath. Ongka stared at the rock. He pronounced: "Avamish." The other two elders nodded reverently and repeated in chorus: "Avamish."

Ongka developed a somber expression. He made motions with his hands that Paul did not understand. It seemed he was indicating something covered, something finished. Yet, something in the intensity with which he regarded Paul, holding his disk, told Paul that the story of Avamish was far from finished. Ongka rose, covering his disk with both hands. The two elders rose, and apparently the interview was over. Paul shook his head slowly, watching the three alien men walk away. What was it they knew? What was it they thought of when they spoke with him of the stars and the planets and of Avamish?

The sun drew to its zenith in the sky. The heat and light of summer burned through the green leaves. The kiln smoked and smelled savory. Villagers straggled down to eat, leaving their planting or harvesting work on the hillsides. Paul pulled Licia aside. She was eating from a scorched leaf. "Well," she said, "you did sleep a long time. Do you feel rested?"

"I was drugged."

"I was too, darling. I haven't slept this well in a thousand years."

"This place is full of surprises." A woman brought him a great-smelling leaf with steam curling from its folds. He didn't know how to go about telling her what he'd learned from the medicus. He'd try when they were alone.

She embraced him. "Paul, honey, I thought you were just sleeping. Sick, maybe. They assured me you would be all right."

"They assured you? How did they do that, in Franglo or Rockie Spanic?"

"Why Paul." She looked at him in genuine surprise. "I'm learning their language."

He laughed, softening, "You're a wonder." He gave her tattered flight suit a look askance, and looked ruefully down at himself. "Can you ask them if there is hot water for bathing?"

She laughed out loud. "Sure! And we have our own bungalow already." Her laughter was a carefree, uncomplicated gesture, as everything on N60A appeared to be.

He started uncomfortably: "Lish, it's all too sweet and easy. We're missing the other two parties, and I feel as though we are being toyed with. I want to get to that city. I want to learn what's going on here."

She touched his cheek with a reproachful finger, "What did we come here for, Paul?"

The word inside, Conquest, did not want to let itself be spoken.

"See—you don't really know. We're here to have children, to give them a better life than we had on Earth. Don't you see, Paul? This is a good place."

"It's a good place all right, like a sponge, soaking you up."

Several young women stared at them from a distance. They waited for Licia to come back and play with their babies. He shooed them off. They retreated with flashing white teeth and dark eyes. "How long did I sleep?"

"Almost two days, Paul,"

"Gawd. Any sign of the Wengs or the Tynans?"

"No."

"And you want to take it easy?"

"Relax, Paul. They know this world a lot better than we do. I've already told them all about our companions."

"We're supposed to sit and wait?"

"That's what they told me while you were asleep."

He softened. "Are they a lot like us, Lish? Do they marry?"

She grinned. "Several teenage boys have already sent me flowers."

"I guess I'd better watch my step,"

"I'd say so."

He put his arm around her and squeezed. "Okay, you win. For now."

That afternoon, Licia showed him the nursery. Several old women tended the village's children. Licia rocked a squalling tiny infant, quieting it with songs in a language from a thousand years ago and light years away. The baby snuggled against Licia and quieted, filling the nursery with peace. Soon, Licia gave the baby up to its mother and joined Paul outside.

Paul and Licia explored around the village. Outside Akha's cultivated hills, the countryside was grassy veldt dotted with clumps of trees as they had traveled through. Ongka and the villagers were busy harvesting apple-like fruits from their orchards. They paid scant attention to the two visitors.

Paul and Licia made love in a field of tall wheat away from the village. After resting a while, they explored further. No wild animals were evident except very small rooting ones. They were becoming inured to the sight of tiny birds, and stopped flinching at the thought of avians bearing down with huge talons and reptile-like eyes.

A low hill about a half mile away drew Paul's attention. Carrying his rifle in hand, he waded through waist-high grass with Licia close behind. The hill was built up artificially with large stones. A fragment of ancient cobblestone road led right up to it, disappearing under its bulk. "A cemetery mound?" Paul wondered.

"No," she said, "they bury their dead on the other side of the village in individual graves. This is something entirely different. But what?"

They lingered about the mound, soaking in its atmosphere of ageless silence and mystery.

It was dusk when they returned to the village. The workers were already sated from a meal around the kiln. Apples were strewn everywhere. The air was heavy with a nectarine aroma. Paul and Licia ate a meal of roasted meat and fruits.

"I remember now."

"What, Paul?"

"The orbital survey. This planet is a huge ball of silica, almost devoid of metals. There's an iron core, but its beyond reach of pick and shovel. Now that I think of it, Ongka's disk is made of copper. That makes it all the more special—and mysterious."

Licia sat cross-legged beside him. Something alien bellowed in the distance, but the villagers were barely distracted. "They have a stone age culture, Paul."

"I can't wait to get a look at that city. How could a stone age planet have a star port? How could they have sent the messages that got us here?"

"Unless we came to the wrong place."

"No, SheuXe and Mannering wouldn't be wrong about something like that." As N60 dropped below the horizon, the temperature dropped noticeably. Licia started to shiver. Paul felt a faint, aching loneliness despite having her curled up beside him.

The villagers laughed and cheered. A group of hunters returned through the orchards, from a long journey, and they called for food. The villagers exclaimed for joy—women for their mates, children for their fathers. The hunters were scratched and muddy. The hunks of game they brought got tucked into crevices inside the kiln for smoking and preservation.

Ongka's disk flashed in the last sunlight. The hunters gathered around him. They all spoke at once, and he held up a hand for silence. Lying at his feet was a prize brought by the hunters. Paul's heart pounded as he drew near. Ongka slowly held the object up in the firelight. It was part of an instrument panel from a lifeboat. Paul recognized the manufacture. The plex dials were still intact. Paul pushed his way through the crowd to touch the object. It could only have come from one of the lifeboats.

Far away, something dreadful bellowed.

Ongka gave Paul a strangely troubled look, holding the panel with mixed aversion and curiosity. Ongka asked a question of the hunters. They danced about, pointing toward the horizon. Ongka explained to Paul that there were more hunters coming, and they brought a person like them with them. A man or a woman, Paul asked. A man, Ongka signed. What man, Paul asked. Ongka signed he did not know more. Soon they would find out. Wait.

Paul found Licia near the kiln. The light flickering on her stressed features told him she had understood the conversation. They were unable to speak.

He went off by himself in the dark. The two moons shone like wet pebbles in the sky. The distorted constellations flowed in the clear night sky like strings of glass beads. Paul sat on a big stone. He almost felt again the delirium-inducing potion that had awakened deep feelings in him. This new horror was like a continuation of the dark dreams after Ongka's look into his soul. This, on top of the fact that they walked on a world full of half-buried ruins, tilted stone mounds, and overgrown roads, peopled by a simple folk who however understood the geography of their solar system and of the Milky Way. Paul could not shake the burning vision of Ongka's face against the background of that infinitely complex, somber clockwork whose gearwheels, cogs, and trip hammers all seemed to work against each other and yet, taken as a whole, displayed perfect harmony.

Returning to Licia's side, he curled up and tried to sleep. Far off, a dog screamed. A bird or small animal warbled sleepily in the underbrush. Alien leaves rustled against each other. Through the doorway, he stared into the blue-black night sky as if into a deep sea. The two silver moons clung together as if they, too, had come here alone from a far and forever lost place and were afraid. Afraid? Tears streamed down Paul's face. Afraid. He again faced fully his own isolation. He dreaded the thought of losing her.

A billion billion leaves rustled against each other like a clockwork, and the wax on their solar surfaces glinted dully in the double moonlight.

During the night, a runner came to the village.

Paul, sleeping beside Licia, awoke when Ongka shook him. Ongka's dark face glistened by torch light. Licia slept fitfully on. The village steeped in cold, pitch-dark silence. Paul wrapped a soft native blanket about his torso and stepped outside. Whispering and gesticulating, Ongka communicated that a ship from the sky had crashed near the village of Shka several days' steady running along the post road. A party from Shka had already left for Akha, bringing Akha hunters and a man with a hurt leg, on a stretcher. Tynan, from the description. Paul grasped Ongka's shoulder. The woman! The woman! What of her?

Ongka motioned that the villagers of Shka had buried a tall, thin woman with long hair yellow as sunlight. The woman looked as if she were asleep. Her eyes were closed, and her cheeks were rose tinged. But cold, oh how cold. Very sad.

Paul returned inside. Without waking Licia, he curled up and remembered the group they had once been. SheuXe and his senior scientists had hand-picked all 18 original candidates for the great journey. All the hours spent discussing, training, theorizing, laughing, sweating, yes, and fighting, cursing, arguing like wild beasts. Under SheuXe's watchful and inscrutable gaze. One by one, they'd been dismissed, until there were six: Paul and Licia, gentle Ping Weng and brilliant Meiling, and then Robert and Mary Tynan. Each couple were spoused, in the Aerie tradition, not married for life, but paired for best evolutionary and survival advantage. Just as unspousing Licia from her father had brought final ruination upon Krings, so Tynan's pairing with Mary wasn't working right. Paul never really understood why. Mary was a smart, very attractive freckled redhead with a love of sports and a good sense of humor. But she was gentle, too, and the competitive Tynan evidently lost patience or desire for her. At first, Paul and Robert had avoided each other. Then, as the others dropped out from day to day, Paul and Tynan (he hated the name Robert and insisted on being called by his last name, which he said sounded tougher and more manly) came into closer orbit of one another. It became clear that Tynan was shooting head-on to spouse Licia for himself. Given her naive nature and her strong drives, and Tynan's will to succeed, Tynan had nearly gotten there. It was the thing about her that Paul hated. He himself had suppressed something of a crush for Mary, though it hadn't been enough to threaten unspousing Licia. Paul and Licia could have been on the verge of breaking up, which would have meant, under harsh Aerie law, that she and Tynan would be spoused, and both Paul and Mary would be separately dropped from the program. As it turned out, a new woman appeared on the scene—Nancy, a niece of Dr. Mannering. Right off, Nancy became the alpha woman. She was taller, blonder, more athletic, smarter, and wiser than all the rest. Overnight, Mary was quietly dropped and disappeared from the group's large but spartan overcondos. Overnight, too, Tynan turned his full attention on Nancy. No doubt SheuXe, Mannering, and the Council had reacted drastically and effectively to the crisis, for Paul and Licia were SheuXe's favorites. Soon, the team had been culled down to the final six pioneers. They'd worked and trained together well now that they were in balance.

From the description Ongka had relayed, it was the Tynans' lifeboat that had gone down near Shka, and it was Nancy who had not survived. Poor Nancy. She had become the player that held the team together. Where Licia could be terribly stubborn, even spoiled, and where Meiling could be teasing or incisive, Nancy had this simple, playful companionableness that was most endearing. Tynan had loved her dearly, and Paul dreaded facing him. The strength of that love had carried the team through any crushing rivalries. It had been a close six-some. Paul and Tynan had even gone hunting together once or twice, while Ping kept more to his medical computers. In all, the group had formed individual friendships with SheuXe, the great genius of his age, and each of the pioneers brought a reverent something of the old man to this new world. Paul longed to put his piece together with the others'. Licia and Nancy had maintained a fairly close friendship. The news would tear Licia up. Meiling had maintained separate friendships with each of the two women. With Licia, Meiling's friendship had been an adolescent one, filled with whispered conversations and giggly conspiracies. Somehow, the six of them became a close-knit team with just the right balance in all things.

17. New World—Year 3301

Tynan arrived at Akha just after dawn. Four men from Shka carried him in a crude sedan chair rigged from wood staves and heavy rope. Tynan's face was mired in grief. Paul helped him to the ground, where Tynan sat and wept without restraint. The natives stood somberly by.

Licia embraced Tynan, rubbing his shoulders and crying with him. Paul offered something to eat, which had been handed to him by a village woman.

Tynan was strong and heavy. A bit later, he grimaced as he shifted his short, broad body. Paul and Licia helped him to stand. A villager offered a stout wooden staff for a primitive crutch. Evidently he had learned about this world's communal kilns. By now he was cried out and silent, though grief had changed his face. He seemed wiped out, blanched, pale, a ghost of himself.

The villagers hovered helpfully about, bringing tea and food. Ongka's old wife knelt by him, offering a bowl of warm water, and a cloth to wipe his face. Tynan thanked her. He ate little. He put the food aside and spoke rapidly, almost hysterically, with a dry flushed face. "Sprained my ankle during the crash. I hit my head going in. I woke up twisted around in the seat. All the plugs and wires had ripped off me. A thousand years, Paul. She lived through it, Paul. We made love one more time, up in the mother ship. A thousand years, then she goes and dies on me." He turned his face away and sobbed. Licia put an arm around his shoulders. He continued: "She died during the crash. I got knocked around and when I came too, she was already dead. I crawled through the wires and junk and tried to revive her. She was dead, like marble, cold. We landed nose down in a swamp. Busted us up. Slammed things around inside of her. Ripped up her organs, I think, splashed her brain against the inside of her forehead, broke her neck as it snapped forward. But she looked like she was asleep, oh God, she looked like she was asleep." Tynan turned his head aside.

The villagers dispersed. Ongka gave curt, loud orders. Paul and Licia helped Tynan hobble to the hut, where Tynan fell heavily onto Paul's cot. Tynan did not seem to want to be alone. Paul and Licia sat beside him. He talked in a stream: "Dogs. Pack of them followed us when we were on our way here, me and the blue folk here. The natives scared the dogs off. Kind of animal whose neck you want to wring on sight."

"You ought to rest," Paul said.

Tynan's eyes were large and bright. "Turtles though, the size of tanks. I saw a herd of them, big green burping things."

Licia went to the kiln to get some hot water that the villagers kept in clay pots.

"I'm so sorry," Paul said when he and Tynan were alone.

Tynan's broad face was red and wet. "She was a wonderful woman."

"Yes. We all loved her."

"I know you did."

"She was wonderful." Part of Paul thought: you were going to take Licia from me and I would have killed you (would I? would I have done that? we'll never know) but the wise people acted fast and intelligently to balance the team.

"I'm not going to let her down," Tynan said, gripping Paul's arm. "We're going to make our lives here work, Menard. The hell with the dogs, the natives, the damn lot. We're going to make it work."

"We have to," Paul said. "It's our mission. We owe it to the people we left behind." First thing they'd done on waking from their sleep had been to listen for transmissions from Earth. There hadn't been any. All they could do was listen—the signal would be 25 years old if there were any. The people back there would know where to broadcast. There was no signal. Earth was another Venus.

Paul looked out and saw Licia walk along the winding hard-beaten earth path carrying a steaming jug. How pure and clean her skin was, how glossy her hair, how bright her eyes, how life played through her eyelashes.

"There are ruins here," Tynan said.

"Yes, I know. We were on the post road."

"It's more than that by far, Menard. A whole lost civilization. I saw ruins all along the way."

Licia entered and began to apply steaming cloths to Tynan's ankle.

Tynan forced a grin. "We'll find that city. We'll explore it. We'll find out what they knew about the stars."

"Sure," Paul said, "we sure will."

Laughter echoed down from the orchards. Tynan quietly fell asleep. His smudged cheeks and hollow eyes looked serene. The sun shone warmly as a cat-thing with yellow eyes, thick brown paws, and no tail crept past. Smoke dribbled over the kiln's chimney. A baby squalled, soon stilled by a kiss or laid against a woman's breast.

Licia rose and motioned as if dusting herself off. "I'm going to the nursery,"

Paul knew better than to say anything.

18. New World—Year 3301

Paul's thoughts drove him out of the village and into the wild places.

The village seemed lost in its bowl of earth. Its sounds were muffled in the high grass. Only a meandering smoke plume from the kiln told him where the village was.

He walked faster and faster, and N60A seemed somehow primordial. The sky was big and blue, and greenery dazed the senses, like on Earth before the clouds. Insect and animal life were in summer abundance. Paul felt free, momentarily, from the pressure building in the village.

Checking his gun with a thought to roaming dogs, he walked toward the mound he and Licia had discovered. Nearby, a shallow forest glowed bright green and was noisy with twittering birds. From the village, faint echoes of voices and tools village blended sweetly with the rustling and twittering of the forest. In midafternoon Paul stood atop the mound. Its eastern, nightward side already fell into shadow. Small, round bushes clung atop the mound with gnarled, anxious roots. All around was the sea of tall grass, of trees, of hidden life—of secrets from the ancient Senders who had inadvertently convinced Earth to send its last six souls here.

Out of the corner of his eyes, Paul thought he caught a flash of light. He whirled, and saw a dark figure standing about a hundred yards away. Ongka. The medicus walked toward the mound without greeting. Paul felt exposed, caught. Did the mound have some religious significance, some taboo, he had missed? No chance to dissemble as Ongka walked toward him.

Ongka stopped at the foot of the mound and looked Paul full in the face. Paul noted the graying skin, the small narrow nose, the curvy mouth, the sharp dark eyes. Ongka's disk flashed as he walked. Paul tried to decipher the look on Ongka's face. Reproachful? But there was an immensely deeper, more melancholy something there. Not taboo, but something whose truth glowed all around them with some subvisible wavelength of revelation, something lost, a matter of long-ago glory, of vain aspiration.

Paul stood stock-still smelling the sweetness of the juice in the grass boiled to a vapor under the pressing sunlight, and watched with hypnotic fascination as Ongka fingered the disk at his chest so that the sun flashed, flashed, flashed.—

—Again, Ongka hovered over him, probing, looking for something in the depths of Paul's soul. The clockwork was there again as their minds met in dim telepathy. Ongka showed no malice, only deep, shuddering questioning, a sympathetic examination. This time, the sharing of the minds was almost equal. Each looked into the other's core. They were alien to each other. Each worked in different realms of abstract thought. Each could only wonder at the other's sense memories. Behind the pictures, Paul knew there was a tremendously intelligent mind operating on abstract paths incomprehensible to himself. Paul could feel Ongka's frustration. What was Ongka looking for? The pleasures, the horrors, the cuddlings, all the clutter of Paul's past? Paul felt more at ease than the previous time, when Ongka had drugged him. Timorously, he peeled away the sheets and sheets of images floating in Ongka's mind. What was this?—the blast and shudder of a huge rocket; pictures of a planet seen from orbit; the densely arrayed stars, the constellations. Somehow, Paul knew it was not the picture he had in his mind, the memory of the mother ship. Judging by the continents below, the planet of orbit was N60A. The pictures fluttered and became indistinct. Ongka was very excited. He'd seen something in Paul that he recognized: the orbital picture of N60A. Paul desperately rifled through the flitting shards of pictures trying to establish a link between Ongka's orbital picture and anything, anything that would explain how this stone-age man could possibly know about such things.

Nothing presented itself. Ongka and Paul were deadlocked, baffled. In the quirky world of this dim telepathic hypnosis, bafflement quickly turned into fear, then into terror. Paul struggled to get away from the alienness; Ongka, too, struggled, though he had not lost control...:*:*:imago mundi:*:*:...Ongka's mind closed up; like a pond, bombarded with light, stood clear and revealed deep, swimming life, but now the angle of light abruptly changed, so that the pond's surface turned opaque and unreadable.

Paul saw the swirl of his own mind reflected on the quivering, rippling surface of the pond of Ongka's mind...:*:*:cathedrals, pyramids, symphonies, sextants, legions, Giant White Condors, millions of acres of snow torn by mountain claws... :*:*:...When Paul awoke, Ongka was gone. Paul was alone on the mound, and an evening chill set in as the first stars appeared in the heavens. He knew only that he and Ongka were not done with this thing—not by a long shot.

19. Old World—Year 2299

The whirlybird chopped steadily over the sun-glazed ice. Its pilot was one of the Aerie's two hundred constables in powder-blue jumpsuit uniform. She steered cautiously around crags where showers of icy grit whirled, forming new slopes of snow.

Wizened little Dr. SheuXe stared tensely from the cocoon of his snow suit, teeth gleaming as if he were smiling. Which most certainly he was not.

Paul, 20, Citizen Constable Intern, rode on the fold-out stool behind SheuXe and the pilot. He had the honor of serving as SheuXe's special assistant on this case. Paul's uniform was so new that it still bore creases from the quartermaster's shelves. Paul resented the fact that they—the Council and its committees—had decided he should do his generalist internship as a constable instead of one of the technical specialties as he had always dreamed. At the moment, he wasn't thinking of that, only of two things—that this ride was his first act of duty as a man and constable; and that the Citizen Anthropologist Rondo Chavez had made a discovery SheuXe said boded the worst danger yet for mankind, a final nail in the coffin of Krings's dream to return to the surface, and the ultimate impetus to begin an interstellar project using old CANUSAMEX hardware left in orbit over the centuries.

A ride on a chopper was a rare treat, even for a constable. Fuel was scarce, coming from several small oil wells on the plateau and slopes just below cloud level. The drillmen, as the oil miners were known, had to wear atmosphere suits near the wells. The aircraft were at least 150 years old, kept patched from a virtually inexhaustible supply of parts stored in the Aerie's subterranean caverns. A lot of equipment still bore old legends like UNASA or CANUSAMEX.

The chopper headed south along the major plateau on which the Aerie had been built. After ten minutes, the pilot veered west and continued along a series of snow-capped peaks. Paul's stomach tensed. He had been told that Rondo Chavez's find was to remain a secret known only to the ruling council, and just the necessary members of the constabulary.

Rondo Chavez! The charming 33-year-old historian had over the years captivated the Aerie's imagination with his stories, slides, and motion pictures. He seemed always to be off on some danger-filled expedition, and one did not need to stray far from the Aerie for that. Initially a disciple of Krings, he had drawn the inevitable conclusions and switched to the space camp of people like Mannering and Souspolitis.

In the chopper, SheuXe said to his pupil Paul: "Now remember everything you ever learned about evolution. Remember what you learned about environment causing viable and lethal mutations. Think of the giant birds we now see." At that, he smiled mysteriously to himself, and it was not a pleasant smile. "Call it competition."

The chopper rocked sharply in a gust of wind. Right ahead was the bright orange marker set up by Rondo Chavez's expedition. The pilot flew over a vast chasm of white ice toward a broad shelf that had several black dots on it. As they drew near, Paul began to make out shapes.

The chopper set down. As the lift surfaces feathered, Paul realized with nausea that the transparent bags on the ice contained the bodies of Rondo Chavez and the members of his expedition. All four men had been stoned to death. Their dead faces—eyes and mouths wide open—radiated the horror of their last minutes.

Mannering and several other Council members were already present. They'd set up an ops-HQ in Rondo's dark blue nylon tent. At least a dozen constables were working on the case, treating it as a multiple homicide. Mannering took SheuXe's arm and helped the elderly man out of the chopper. SheuXe shook his arm free and pointed along a path that led in among the mountain uplifts. Mannering summarized: "We think they caught Rondo and his men by surprise. First they started throwing stones from the tops of those cliffs. The men managed to drag themselves over to where we found them, trying to radio for help. Then the bastards ran up close to finish them off right where they are lying now."

Paul noted that two dozen more constables with shotguns stood all about the high points. Sun gleamed on the face shields of their helmets. Two of them shouted a conversation with two others below. Mannering spoke urgently with SheuXe, who summoned Paul to help him climb among the rocks. It was dark between the stone faces, and colder than any refrigerator. How could life exist in such a place? A gentle wind keened and moaned through the passages, making Paul's hair stand on end. He kept imagining he heard whispers just around this or that corner. He kept one hand under SheuXe's elbow, the other on his loosened holster. SheuXe was old and fragile, but he was a wisp of a person, and therefore supple. With his walking stick, and Paul and Mannering helping him, they descended down a winding path. Snow crunched around their boots. Their breathing came in ragged strokes, lost in the music of the air.

There was a cave opening. Inside it was dry and dark, and not quite so cold. A battery-powered lamp stood on a tripod to shed light on the interior. Paul smelled a strong, stale odor that was unlike anything he'd ever smelled before. Neither avian nor human, but definitely spoor-marking. The cave was a dead end, a rough circle some 30 feet across. It had been scooped out eons before by side pressure from an arm of a receding sea as the land pushed up.

"How many?" SheuXe asked.

Mannering considered. "Maybe a half dozen. We're bringing dogs in. But there may be many more than that scattered far out of our reach."

"We can keep them away from us, but for how long?" SheuXe said. His shocked, thin, spectacled face radiated the additional realization that he wouldn't be around much longer to lead the fight. He was dying from cancer of the throat, having been a lifelong smoker of the golden tobaccos grown on the sunward slope. He'd called it his only vice.

In the center of the cave Paul saw the remains of a campfire. The fire had been made with wood, bits of coal, and some form of animal oil as the stains on the wood showed. Mannering pointed to some strawy biscuits. "Those are the droppings of mountain grazers, goats probably. They burn long and hot. You can make a good fire with those. And anything else you can find."

The cave entrance was like a cleft lip, providing a natural flue. Dry, cracked bits of bone lay scattered around the fire—someone or something's lunch. Paul thought he recognized the bones of a small mountain hen, cracked and sucked empty of their marrow.

Mannering pointed to a hole at the far end of the cave. Paul smelled a faint odor of dead flesh. "This is what Rondo Chavez had discovered, when they killed him. It's a burial pit."

Inside the pit lay a small, strange skeleton, neither human nor animal. It was about four feet tall, Paul guessed, and still had most of the blackened flesh attached due to the cold. At first Paul thought it was a chimp, but then he could see the face was all wrong. It had remnants of reddish hair along the head. Its body had been slightly flattened by the heavy load of gravel and earth used to fill the grave above it. The creature had long, spindly arms and legs sort of like a monkey perhaps. Wrapped around one wrist was a leather thong, and at the end of the thong was a little leather pouch as yet unopened; food, perhaps, for the afterlife.

"What is this thing?" Paul asked.

SheuXe had already formed his opinion. "It's a bat, Paul. An evolved, intelligent bat, and its relatives have killed their first humans."

Paul stared at the large leathery wings folded on the creature's back, from the neck down to the thighs. There was something intelligent, pondering, and ominous as it lay on its side, curled eternally in a fetal position, awaiting the coming of the sun. Or the rising of the moon.

20. New World—Year 3301

Paul felt drained. and dizzy on the mound, alone after Ongka's disappearance. Dreamily, Paul stumbled through the quickly deepening twilight toward the village. In his mind remained an afterglow of his second mind exchange: of a buried civilization that had once ruled this planet; that had, a thousand years earlier, broadcast news of its glory to all the galaxy.

The last moments of the sun glowed sadly on the post road into the village. The work on the hillsides was finished and the villagers thronged about their smoky kiln. The aroma of food and smoke filled the sunken village. In it mingled new smells: apples and cider.

Paul found Licia and Tynan sitting on a log with at least a dozen bouncing, excited little naked children, He saw no trace of Ongka. Tynan sat gloomily beside her, eating from the customary dish—a leaf. Licia's face glowed with pleasure as she played with the children. She absently put one arm around Paul.

The villagers had given Tynan a hut of his own, further down the lane. When they were alone together, Paul told Licia of his second encounter with the medicus.

She flipped her hair back. "You two seem to be getting along rather well." Seeing his annoyed look, she added: "Paul, I don't know if you're dreaming these things up or what. Can't you just loosen up and enjoy life a little bit?"

"I've told you already," he said. "I don't want to sit in this place and go soft. We came here for a reason."

"We survived!" she shouted after him as he left. "Isn't that enough for one thousand years?"

He went to the kiln and helped himself to a leaf full of cinnamony rice paste and a cup of hot water with a few minty leaves in it. Then he sat on a low wall and ate. Still annoyed at Licia, and muzzy from the hypnosis, he watched disinterestedly as a runner came down into the village. It was a young boy, who ran straight to Ongka's hut.

The medicus stepped forth a moment later. Ignoring Paul, as if they didn't know each other, Ongka went to the center of the square and waited. Paul's attention perked up. A small group of men and women came down into the village along the post road. Several walked in pairs. Each pair carried between them a pole slung over one shoulder, and wrapped around the pole a blanket or canvas with objects in it. What caught Paul's attention most, though, was the young woman walking in their midst. She was very young, perhaps in her late teens. She was a bit taller than most of the women Paul had seen. Her skin was of plum complexion, somewhere between brown and blue. She wore the common long skirt; and a jacket buttoned to the neck, made of soft sandy-colored leather embroidered with multicolored beadwork. She had silvery hair on her head almost in a page boy style. She carried herself simply and upright, holding a staff in one slender hand, and she was beautiful. The young woman smiled dazzlingly as Ongka greeted her. Ongka embraced her and took her into his hut. Three young men who had come with her stayed outside the hut with spears to guard her.

It wasn't until the next evening as the village sat around dinner, and as musicians played string instruments and sang a softly lilting harmony, that Paul noticed the young woman again. She had just slipped through the crowd, making the customary offerings of tea to anyone who needed a refill, and now she stood before Tynan. She took Tynan's cup and poured into it from a steaming jug. Tynan stared away, obviously wishing she would leave him alone. The girl smiled shyly and held the cup before Tynan's face. Tynan looked down into the cup, which smelled of pleasant herbs, looked at her, and sighed. Beaming, the girl brought the same offer of hospitality to Paul and Licia.

"Her name is Auska," Licia said, "She is Ongka's niece, Pretty, isn't she?"

"Thanks," Paul told Auska, and she inclined her face before pulling away. She seemed about eighteen. Today she wore a matching outfit of plain white cotton sling top and skirt-like garment that fell very loosely to the knees and could be tucked between the thighs when kneeling to work. Auska's long, thin torso made her look even younger by Earth standards. There was something girlish about her, something elastic to her back when she sat. Her silvery hair gleamed in the twilight, as did her straight teeth and the whites of her eyes. Her breasts were small and high-set; her facial features were squarer and more similar to his and Licia's than Paul had realized, except her eyes were faintly elongated straight-out rather than slanted. She had an intelligent, sensitive, humorous face, fitting for Ongka's niece.

The villagers began a big party. Dozens of white smiles and swaying bodies accompanied the increasingly loud music. String, drums, and flutes sounded thin and persistent, with an airy gaiety. In the cool, sweet dusk, bonfires blazed along the post road. Paul drank fruity liquor from a wooden cup until he became mildly drunk. All of Akha cheered, including the children.

21. Old World—Year 2299

"I just had a call from up range," Mannering said as Paul and SheuXe stood staring at the mummy in the grave. "Come on, quick!"

They followed Mannering's enormous bulk to a chopper. After a short, hectic ride through several treacherous wind pockets that threatened to dash them against the age-blackened rocks, they saw several constables waving. The chopper set down and Paul was the first one out. He wished he had his rifle with him, for he immediately recognized the thrill of the hunt in the young constables' eyes. It was immediately clear to him what had happened. They had driven a group, a family perhaps, of the creatures toward a box canyon. Several had tried to fly out, but they weren't fast enough; their bodies lay sprawled and broken on the teeth of the walls surrounding the canyon. "We got one trapped in there," a constable said.

"Take him alive if possible!" Mannering shouted as he came up at a run. His rifle looked like a toy in his huge hands.

The air here was actually almost warm and smelled noxious. Paul guessed there was a lava vent somewhere nearby, and perhaps that had something to do with the coming of these new creatures. Thunder growled loudly in the cloud sea. Still, the scene wasn't much different from what he'd seen all his life in the Aerie—a thick cover of ashen clouds forming a floor that ran for tens of miles, and above it bright sunshine in the upper atmosphere, and vistas of mountain ranges running as far as they eye could see.

"There!" Paul spotted flashes of movement in the thickets at the edge of the canyon. Paul felt the slow, steady movement as Mannering carefully aimed his trank gun.

Small fur-covered winged creatures ran explosively for cover.

One of the mutants confronted Mannering. The bat-man's wings spread like a fan behind. His spindly arms stretched out in defense of the others. He held a small, metal-tipped spear in one hand. A bag on a thong hung from the other wrist. The red-furred face looked half simian, with a recognizable pride and defiance in the big dark eyes, in the sneering cast of the man-like mouth.

Mannering fired. Once. Twice. The little man looked as though he were going to cry as he dropped his spear and clutched his side where the darts had hit. His face, as he fell, had an accusing look none of the watchers would ever forget. Up on the rim, a fusillade of gunfire erupted as the constables began picking off the other members of the clan, killing them one by one.

"We are no longer alone," Paul heard Mannering say to SheuXe behind himself. "I wonder what else is growing in these mountain peaks."

SheuXe's reply was a whisper, snatched away by the wind, but Paul thought he said: "It's just a matter of time. Just a matter of time."

22. New World—Year 3301

Paul took Licia to their stone house, where they made giddy, woozy love. They laughed together, and their kisses were wet and fruity. Then they returned to the feast.

Tynan drank steadily from a goose-necked jar. Firelight shone on his sweaty face as he watched the dancing. He was surrounded by admiring children. The children, like clay dolls with ivory smiles, avidly demonstrated for Tynan's enjoyment some small dance they made up as they went along. Tynan grinned and raised his cup when he saw Paul and Licia.

Paul noticed a slim figure standing in the shadows, watching the Earth pioneers. Auska. Her look was inscrutable, and Paul had the strange sensation that all three of them were under a microscope.

23. New World—Year 3301

Days went by, droning with bees and rustling with leaves. Weeks went by. Paul counted, growing frantic with impatience. They waited for Tynan's leg to mend. This much Tynan and Licia had agreed on with Paul: that they should try for the city soon. According to Ongka, it was now the end of summer and the height of harvest. Copious amounts of fruity liquor were being distilled from apples and other plants, and the sealed stone jugs piled up in every house including Paul and Licia's. As laborers came in from elsewhere, the village grew short on living space. Tynan was forced to move in with Paul and Licia, which effectively ended their privacy. There was no word of the Wengs yet, none at all, and Paul began to wonder if they'd been killed in a crash. Word was going around the world by messenger. Sooner or later, Ongka promised, the missing couple would be found, if they had survived their landing. In the meantime, the three humans were slowly adapting to the slow, secure village life. They learned snatches of the language. Auska came often to look after Tynan, who alternated between depression and agitation. By now, Licia had gone native, to save her Earth clothes (she said). She had come by some attractive multi-colored sling tops and dresses for helping several women with their children.

One morning, Paul was startled out of his sleep as the door flap opened and the full sun burst in out of a clear sky. "Powul."

"Lish?" A shaft of sunlight blinded him. He reached out and touched a soft face that was not Licia's but Auska's. She offered a jug of water. The cold fluid felt good to his mouth and throat. When he stepped outside, stretching, the morning air was fresh and sweet and full of bird noises. "Powul," Auska said, holding up an implement for digging. "Ongka balawang mPowul mfiglig mflid," she said, or something like that, which he took to mean that Ongka wanted them to work. He pointed questioningly up at the orchards. Not that they hadn't pitched in a little bit, but they'd really been taking advantage, and perhaps now Ongka was giving them the what-for. "Nagi, nagi," Auska said, no, no, "wammang apo Powul shediwid duwidu malacan hamong," she said in their singsong language. She pointed toward the open country and gestured until he understood: Ongka had given them permission to enter the mound.

"Ah, the mound!" He danced about making mound shapes. "The mound!"

"Dafa!" she said brightly. "Dafa! Mowund." She made mound shapes with her arms. Then she pointed at him and laughed teasingly. "Powul mlarn Vamish barr." She pointed to her tongue, which was blue. "Barr."

He pointed into his mouth. "Mouth. Tongue. Barr." He waved a finger in the air. "You'll have me learning your blasted lingo yet!"

She waved her finger in the air and proclaimed: "Mblastod mlingo yut!"

"It's a great day!" Paul shouted, looking for Tynan and Licia. Finally, they were about to make some progress. The medicus wanted to part with what might be a great secret, and Paul couldn't wait. He accepted the digging implement, a stone adze on a wooden handle, and marched out the door. "Tynan!"

Auska disappeared as Tynan hobbled around the corner where he'd been cleaning items in his kit with hot water and a sponge. "What are you shouting about, Menard?"

The tools were crude but bore the luster of precise, loving craftsmanship. Their straight, round wood handles gleamed from much use. The blades of spade and pick were light, strong stone; at first Paul mistook them to be of dark, pitted iron.

Tynan hobbled forth, and Licia joined them from the orchard where she'd been gathering food for the kiln. "Better watch that old shaman," Tynan said looking dubiously at his digging tool.

Licia gave Tynan a saucy look. "I think he wants you to spouse his niece." "You men have fun. I'm going to gather dinner for us. I'll bring it out to you." She strode off, jiggling in her blue and red checked shamiss, as the natives called the dress.

As they passed the kiln, Paul spotted Ongka. The medicus sat impassive with his two cronies. Paul's and Ongka's eyes fleetingly made contact. Ongka was lacing a stone tip to a throwing spear. The normally practiced fingers moved with fleeting but unsteady motions. Ongka noted the digging implements and then concentrated on his handiwork.

As they walked, Paul said: "Soon, Tynan,"

"What?"

"Soon we'll start for Avamish."

"That city gives you no rest."

"We need to find out."

"Find out what?"

"Have you forgotten? The Senders?"

"All right, just take it easy."

They came to the mysterious earthen mound. A silence of lost voices whispered around the structure. The wind, ruffling miles of grass and flowers, told endlessly that the builders of a lost civilization hovered about as ghosts and caprices of ambition and conversation.

Tynan pointed to the horizon. "What do you make of that?"

Paul followed Tynan's direction and spotted several distant figures walking. Tall, dark male shapes. They carried spears and shields and walked single-file. "Looks like a team of warriors," Paul said. "I doubt they're from our village. Wonder where they are going." Paul scrambled up the mound to see better. His motion caught their gaze. As they turned their heads, he saw that each had painted a white stripe from the nose, up the forehead, and running back over the head. They looked eerie as they turned to return Paul's gaze—which suddenly made their whitened faces shine—and just as eerie, they kept walking, like ghosts, winking out of sight into some tall reeds.

"We should probably start here," Paul said, indicating the spot where the ancient cobblestone road disappeared into heaped stones and earth. He felt sweaty as the morning sun burnt down upon them, before they'd begun working.

Paul struck a shaft. He and Tynan alternatingly picked and dug. At first the heavy stones didn't want to yield. Uniformly rectilinear, like twenty pound sugar cubes but gray, they wanted to stick together as they had for hundreds of years.

"These people are going to kill us if they see us doing this," Tynan said at one point.

"We have permission from their medicus."

"I hope you know what you're saying. For all we know, they'll bury us in here."

It was tough going at first. Tynan's leg began to bother him. "Sit down," Paul urged.

"I can't let you—."

"No," Paul insisted, "we need for that leg to heal so we can get going, out of here."

"You and that damn city," Tynan muttered, and he did not sit down, but he did slow the pace of his digging considerably.

Once they got through the outer layer of stones, the going got easier. Crumbly black soil with interlocking roots lay bare before them. A small gray lizard rasped flashing out of its threatened nest and sought refuge in a bush. Slowly turning worms glistened in the freshly cut loam. Out of a broken ball of spit and mud, the size of a man's head, issued a fleeing swarm of tiny white ants.

Paul dug in the direction of the interrupted road, which bared its wet black stones for the first time in centuries.

Toward noon, Licia returned with jugs and bundles, "You two look like you're working hard." She set a neatly wrapped parcel on a rock. "From Mrs. Ongka." Tynan unwrapped the leaves to find a large, wet green melon festooned with crushed flowers.

Paul produced a pocket knife from his flight suit and the melon was sweet and quenching.

Licia stayed a while. "I'm dying to find out what is in that mound. Do you suppose it's a buried king? A treasure? Well, we can't ask Ongka, because he left."

"Left?" Paul was surprised; he'd expected the shaman to hover nervously about, to see if lightning struck the pioneers as they excavated his precious mound.

"He left a little while ago, and it looks like he's off on a long trip. He took twelve men with him, including Dunda and Amda. They were loaded down with supplies, lots of jugs of applejack."

"Let me guess," Paul said, "They headed toward Avamish."

She nodded, "I get the feeling they do it every year or two."

Tynan and Paul both laughed. Tynan said: "They save up their hootch and then go to the big city for a bash."

She gathered her things up, adding primly: "In some primitive cultures, what we consider a bash may be a sacred ritual. I've made a new friend."

"Oh?" Paul arched an eyebrow. "You're going to run off to the city also?"

"Don't be an ass. I started talking with Auska, the chief's niece. She's a very nice girl. She's interested in our language, our customs, she just follows me around everywhere. And, I might add, sometimes another women is better company. Bye." She picked up her basket and strode down the path toward the village.

The afternoon sky grew hazy and hot. Mirages shimmered on the far-off forests where hidden things bellowed. "That sound," Tynan said, "that goddamn sound. I kept hearing it after we hit the water. Sounds like something waiting to eat us." Tynan scraped silently at the dirt beside Paul. "Your woman doesn't want to leave here, Menard. She's happy, and maybe I'm starting to crack a few smiles now and then too. There are some beautiful women here that look like they can—you know what I mean. I don't know if I want to leave here either."

Paul stopped and looked at him. They were both covered with dirt, "Tynan, for God's sake." They looked at each other silently while the lush wilderness about them chirruped sweetly with birds and insects. "Tynan, we have an obligation."

"Spare me the lecture."

By evening they had dug their way to an inner wall of gray stones. Paul was amazed at how the earth was filled with life, squirming with worms, insects, rodents, some similar to earth forms, others utterly alien. Like the gray cube that sat motionlessly brooding in the soil; when you drew close it hissed at you, even spat something sticky and itchy; and beneath its surface you could see tiny running things. He jabbed one open with his spade, and found the running things were vomity looking purplish bean things that rolled through china-fine tunnels like a solid bloodstream.

The summer heat lingered long, drowning in haze. The sun was a tomato dunked in heavy air. Licia appeared. "You should quit for the day."

Paul groaned. "So close."

Tynan agreed. "No lightning bolts yet from any angry gods. I ache, therefore I am. Whatever is in there, it won't go away overnight."

Licia rubbed Paul's back. "You two need a good washing."

With the sun gone, and therefore their light, they walked back toward the village. The temperature dropped noticeably, bringing welcome coolness. The twin moons shone like pitted silver through the tree tops. The sky turned charcoal and stars glimmered. Eternity.

24. New World—Year 3301

"There it is," Paul said, next day. He and Tynan lay side by side on their bellies staring into the interior of the mound. Tynan's flashlight beam was blunted by a dead darkness. Sweat shone on their dirt-streaked faces.

"My God," Tynan said. "What is it?"

Arriving in the fresh morning sunlight, they had first admired how much work they'd accomplished the day before. Then, within an hour, they'd broken through the inner wall, and now they lay in their tunnel looking in.

"It took a lot of work to seal this building," Tynan said. His voice sounded leaden and flat.

"Here goes." Paul climbed in, lowering himself until he felt a firm floor under his feet. "Come on in." Tynan followed suit. It was terribly dry inside.

Their entry had disturbed a fine dust that hung like fog in the motionless air. It made glare of the flashlight beams. Paul pointed to a huge object looming before them. He took a few steps on the dusty floor stones. He brushed away clouds of fine cobwebs. "Look, Tynan, it's a wagon."

They stood side by side and marveled. It was a flat-bedded load wagon some fifteen feet long and half as wide. "This is what the old man wanted us to do all this work for?" Tynan looked disgusted.

"There has to be a reason—look, Tynan, it's made of stone. Can you believe it? A stone wagon!" Paul shook his head slowly. "Hard to believe. Those wheels look smooth as though they were made in a factory. I don't think it's something Ongka's people made."

"Ahhh," said Tynan the engineer. "I begin to get it. They had little or no metal to work with, the old people, the Senders. Solid rock—looks like metal, but it's rock, poured, molded, tenpered, not a slip of metal on this wagon anywhere."

"Or those other tools," Paul said. "Somehow, they used stone the way we did metal."

They walked around the wagon, their flashlights stabbing in all directions. Paul said, "this place may have been a sealed a thousand years ago. But why? Where did the Senders go? Why did they seal everything up, even their tool shed here?" A clutter of large and. small objects loomed in the darkness. Something like the arched ribs of a great animal that had died on its back turned out to be a harvester, made of tempered stone.

Paul remembered a tangle of circles and squares that was Ongka's clockwork.

"There's nothing but stone machines all around us," Tynan said.

"And tools," Paul added. Chains of stone links hung from the walls and from stone supporting pillars. Dry, transubstantiated wisps of straw puffed out of existence under their feet. Paul saw ghostly work benches laden with stone hammers, files, planes, saws, pliers, wrenches, all marvelously smooth and masterfully made.

"This is obsidian," Tynan said full of awe, as he held a small wooden box of blades. "This stuff is stone but can be made sharper than surgical steel. The Maya and the Incas successfully performed brain surgery with it."

There were drills with wooden bits and drills with stone bits, drills with diamond tips and drills. Tynan picked up a drill with the bit still in it. "Corundum, I'll bet. These clever so and sos, they made alloys of stone and stone, and metal and stone. On Earth, we soon graduated to metal alloys. Here they never had that luxury."

Paul considered the implications. "Imagine, a civilization that never left the stone age. On earth we discovered metals. Oh, there was a stone age that lasted many thousands of years. Our early ancestors on Earth had factories where they made stone implements. They discovered metals, though, and that spelled the end of their industry. On this planet, the stone age never ended. They must have explored the limits of what you can do with stone."

"Look at this," Tynan said.

"What is it?" Paul whirled.

Tynan's flashlight stabbed into a hidden corner. There, piled neatly on top of each other, were dozens of skulls. Paul's heart raced as they cautiously stepped closer. The skulls grinning at them must be a thousand years old, black and brittle. Many had severe gouges in them, as if their owners had died violently. Some had their faces bashed into splinters. Other bones lay strewn about—ribs, femurs, fingers. "What do you suppose happened here?" Paul asked.

Tynan shook his head. They stared at the bones until their lights weakened and they had to head back to the daylight. Tynan said at last: "You say Ongka knows about space flight?"

Paul nodded. "For some reason, when they came to the end of their civilization, they sealed up this mound, maybe for us to discover, maybe for us find some way to progress beyond the point where they ran out of steam. And maybe some of them killed some others, for reasons we don't know."

Tynan shook his head slowly. "Menard, quit dreaming. This planet is a giant sandbox. This mound is like a message left for us. A message of despair. What can we do without metals? Do you understand what this means? There is no space-faring civilization. Maybe there was or maybe there wasn't, but there sure hasn't been in centuries. So we're stuck here. There is no way back into space, not tomorrow, not in a million years."

Paul disagreed in turn, turned off by the other's adamant negativity. "Dammit, Tynan, they sealed this place up for a reason. Ongka wanted us to find it this way. I don't feel he's given up." Paul remembered the clockwork, and Ongka's nearly religious fervor, and the medicus' passion about the great city they called Avamish. "We have to go to the star port, Tynan. We have no choice. We have to find out—the sooner the better—what went on here."

Having glimpsed other tantalizing pieces of this puzzle, Paul climbed out of the mound. Tynan crawled out behind him. Leaving the dust and debris of a dead civilization behind them, it felt good to reenter the sunlight of the living. Paul was quietly grateful for the sounds of birds and insects that signified life.

Auska and Licia approached with lunch. As they laughed and conversed, they were making themselves haltingly familiar with one another's languages. They walked together like old friends. Auska, younger than Licia, carried a basket and made hop scotching jumps that Paul found cute. At times, Auska could seem regal; at other times, a child. Licia clowned along, balancing a jug on her head.

Auska forgot her shyness and waved to the two men as if they were old friends. Auska spread a blanket. Licia positioned the jug and laid the picnic basket beside it. Paul sniffed—and exclaimed: "You two smell of wine."

"Applejack," Licia said, offering him a cup. "Go on, it's diluted with water." He sipped from it and felt refreshed. "The whole village smells of this stuff, Paul. They've stopped harvesting and they're now in the distilling business." She giggled.

Auska scrambled squealing up the side of the mound. Tynan went after her, hobbling and grasping. She ran so fast and so eagerly she fell. Up in a blink, she ran to the top of the mound. There she waited, holding two small bottles high over her head. An ivory grin slashed her dusky features. Her bare, slim waist was exposed as her jacket rode up.

Paul nudged Licia. "So what do women on this planet think about things?"

She paused in mid-chew. "About what, men?"

"I dare not ask. About things in general."

"In some ways, she's just like another aerie girl. Then again, in other ways, she is so strange and different that it scares me."

"Like what?"

"Well, she's obviously a chief's daughter. A princess. I gather she is a virgin, and that she is saving herself for a great chief she will marry one day in Avamish."

"You'd better tell Tynan," Paul said, pointing. Tynan was chasing her down the mound. Auska stopped and laughingly fended him off. He tried to embrace her in a gesture probably meant more as mock wrestling. Abruptly, she let out a yell. Her facial expression changed from amused to shocked, and she pushed Tynan away. Tynan tipped over backwards and sat, dumbfounded, watching Auska's pert rear disappear through the bushes toward Akha.

Tynan limped sourly toward Paul and Licia.

"We tried to warn you," Paul said.

"Too late," Licia said. "We learn another lesson about etiquette. You can play with a princess, but you never touch her."

Tynan slapped dust off his trousers and muttered: "Bloody stuck up bitch."

25. New World—Year 3301

When they returned to Akha later in the afternoon, the village stood nearly empty. All the imported workers had returned to their villages elsewhere, now that the harvest was over and the apple wine newly fermented. With Ongka and his entourage gone, it seemed to Paul you could sleep in a different hut each night.

Paul, Licia, and Tynan met for supper at the kiln. There were still enough elderly women to cook a generous meal of at least seven different things, including the local poultry. Auska appeared for dinner, a little more reserved, but not unfriendly. Paul pressed: "Auska—why did Ongka go to Avamish?"

Auska chewed slowly, considering. "Ongka balam ada Avamish."

"Yes. Why?"

"Mbalam le Avamish ni adaram ho tolne abaligung."

Paul enjoyed her singsong speech. He was able by now to pick out a word here and there, and Licia helped fill in, but then she'd rattle on. He'd get so lost in the music of her speech that it would be seconds before he remembered to ask her to stop and start over.

Licia said: "Something about Ongka has to go, it's a great festival."

"Bestibo," Auska said nodding. She set her food down and gestured with delicate brown fingers. "Bestibo s'Avamish malam amanga apat witu moliam." She grew excited and spread her hands in the air. "Moliam witu," she repeated several times making a gesture resembling an explosion. "Astad moliam, witu witu."

"Bang bang," Licia guessed.

Auska choked with pleasure at being understood. She pointed at Licia, nodded, held her hand over her mouth, and cleared her throat.

"Moliam probably means big," Paul guessed. He made circular motions and said: "Moliam!"

Auska nodded. "Moliam witu." She gestured.

Paul stood up and spread his arms as far as he could. "Moliam moliam!"

Auska laughed so hard she nearly fell off the little wall by the kiln. She imitated Paul in return, a glint of humor in her eyes. "Moliam witu. Bang bang. Bestibo bang bang. Ho tolne abaligung." With her index finger she pointed upward and rising, appeared to follow the trajectory of something—upward, upward—she bounced on the balls of her feet, pointing to the evening stars. "Abaligung ho tolne."

Licia marveled, and she said in a whisper: "I think abaligung means heaven."

Paul nodded in agreement. Then a black shudder went through him and he added: "Or outer space?"

"We've got to go to the city," Paul told Licia that night, "we've got to get to Avamish."

She was already half asleep. It was dark in the hut, which reeked of cold, burned tallow. "Paul!" she muttered.

"Licia, don't you remember? We have a mission here. We have to find out all there is to know, as quickly as possible, so we can establish ourselves."

She turned and looked at him. Her eyes glittered angrily, and her face looked pale in the faint starlight. "Are you saying we should take over? Five people—three if we can't find Meiling and Ping Weng—against a whole world?" She sounded pitying.

He could sense an argument about to moliam witu, and he couldn't bear the idea. "All I'm saying is that for our own protection, we need to know—what if these people are planning to eat us when they get us good and fat enough?"

She snorted and turned her back to him.

He felt his handles and then pinched her waist. "We're not getting any thinner hanging around here. We're not asked to work, and we can eat all we want. Maybe we're like pets to them. Like chickens or dogs—."

Licia sat up. "Paul, you sound like an idiot." But he could see from her eyebrows that she was considering this from all angles. He added: "We can always come back here."

"I already know all the children by name."

"We'll be back in a few weeks. It's only a few hundred miles."

"On foot."

"We'll take our time."

"Why don't you go and I'll keep the hut warm."

Hah, he thought, and Tynan would argue that his ankle hurt. "No way, Licia. Either we all go, or we all stay. We stay together."

Tynan laughed at first. "What are you going to do, report me to the constab?"

"I'm saying, we agreed to a mission." They stood face to face outside Tynan's hut. "We made a solemn promise to the rest of our race, who are dead a thousand years now, that we would keep our people going."

Tynan sighed. "All right. How can I say no to that?"

They found Auska sitting with Licia in Ongka's hut. Auska was showing Licia how to make fancy knots using the dyed leather strips that decorated her best shamiss. As Paul stuck his head into the hut, Licia nudged Auska. Licia had a sparkle in her eye. Auska pointed her chin at Paul. "Waad joo beeg ape?"

Paul choked with laughter.

Tynan pointed his thumb at Paul. "This man wants to go to Avamish."

Licia made a face, but Auska jumped up. "Mbalagang Avamish?"

"Paul," Licia said wearily.

"Will your spouse agree to go?" Tynan asked Paul.

"I'm not sure."

Tynan grinned. "Well, you'd better be sure."

Auska began throwing possessions in a leather bag. "Mbalag ampat Avamish nioske!"

Paul knelt by his spouse. "Licia, the others are willing to go. We can only go if you agree to go with us. We have to stick together. Auska will guide us. She has several men who will walk with us."

Licia hesitated. "Paul, I think it's a mistake to leave here. But yes, I will come along. I don't know why. Maybe it's because I love you. Or because it's our duty. Or both." She kissed him, then stepped out of the hut to put her things together.

They started out just after dawn the next day. The rising sun's rays streaked horizontally through the barely moving leaves. Fog drizzled ephemerally in the stone village and along the post road, diffracting sunlight into tiny rainbows while birds chattered.

"I'm more worried about the dogs than anything," Paul said. They sported their weapons openly. They'd packed just enough to travel light, including some dried fruits and meats that the kiln ladies had packed for them.

Auska walked ahead, accompanied by Licia and three young men wearing the tan skirts and jackets of the village from which Auska came, two days' march east. Today they headed another way, toward Avamish. There seemed to be no warriors here, but they carried spears and knives. They were hunters, Paul supposed.

At times Licia and Auska dropped back to talk with Paul and Tynan. At other times they walked ahead. The three young hunters appeared to be in good humor, occasionally fortifying themselves with apple wine. This was a big adventure for them, Paul guessed, because Licia said none had ever been to Avamish.

Tynan's leg didn't bother him anymore. Licia had rediscovered her sense of adventure. For now, at least, his little party hung together nicely. Should they ever return to Akha? Was Licia's instinct to nest here correct? No way of knowing until they'd visited the planet's only great city. And what about the things that hollered in the forest? Were they a threat, or just background music? There was a lot they must learn.

The road stretched on arrow-straight. In a few spots it sank down into earth, sometimes under a momentary carpet of soil rich with grass and flowers. The countryside was grassy and hilly, dotted with lakes. Herds of the high-haunch buffalo passed in the distance. Once they saw a distant pack of dogs, but the dogs tracked something away toward the horizon.

"Look!" Paul said, pointing with his rifle. Not far away, near a pond covered with water flowers, stood a pink and green tortoise twelve feet long and eight feet high.

"I remember seeing those on the way to Akha," Tynan said. They headed toward Shka, where Nancy lay buried, and Paul wondered how Tynan would take that.

More of the disdainfully munching giants dotted the lush plain.

"Like war tanks," Licia whispered as they passed the first giant. It was the biggest of the herd, and it had tusks. They guessed that it must be the bull of the herd. As they passed, it flicked out its tongue with a hissing sound. Its fan shaped tongue was fringed with curling tendrils that knotted themselves around greens so the animal could tear them off.

"Sorry," Paul told the closest turtle. "We'd love to spend a day studying you but we're on a mission."

Tynan said: "I hope the bastards don't stampede. I can't run so well yet."

"If they stampede," Licia said, "we'll all be riding high."

"On top of those horns." They laughed. The young men joined the laughter without understanding it. The turtles were evidently a common subject for jokes on N60A.

The countryside gave way to forest.

The post road continued straight on, through a chapel-like peace. Paul was in high spirits, having at last freed himself of Akha. The dense, glowing forest was filled with whispers and stolen sunlight. No more turtles. Nothing bellowing, and Auska did not exhibit any particular fear.

A big gray cube of concrete loomed in the woods, in a culvert off to the right side of the road. Paul clambered down while Tynan and the women remained warily on the road. The young men grew apprehensive, jabbering darkly and pointing their spears. "Nagi," they shouted, "nagi! Nagimo."

Tabu, Paul guessed. In the end, Auska and Licia calmed them. Paul climbed down the embankment himself.

As he neared the box-shaped structure, he and a fox-like animal surprised each other. The animal disappeared in a streak of reddish hackles. Paul waited for his heart to resume a normal beat. Rifle ready, he walked to the doorway. Outside, the structure was overgrown with rich pads of blue and green moss. The walls, which might once have been smooth gray or even off-white, were now blackened with age. Flat-layered, pink mushrooms grew along the edges like coral. A yellow lizard scuttled up the wall; on its fat custard-colored back was a large eye whose pupil coldly tracked Paul while its owner ran for safety. He clambered over boulders and fallen trees toward the utilitarian building.

The one-room structure was gloomy inside, filled with an apparitional green light. Water dripped loudly. Insects plagued Paul's face. Inside were the remains of some complex stone machine, looming to just under where the ceiling had once been. The marshy black ground was filled with shattered bits of clay pipe, some of it slimmer than a man's finger. Fat pieces of stone conduit were filled with a dozen or more spaghetti-thin ceramic pipettes.

Each pipette had a stained, needle-thin bore. Paul picked up a few fragments to show the others.

He returned to the road above.

The three young hunters stood sullenly in a group up the road.

Tynan held up two pieces, one with a male thread, the other flared and female, and examined them. "The stains probably indicate some sort of fluid, maybe an oil, Lord knows for what purpose." He took his knife and chipped a diagonal cut into one piece. "They're the size of electrical wires, except of course there is no conductor inside because they had very little metal."

Paul pointed, "There are remnants of conduit running parallel to the road as far as I can see."

Tynan threw the pieces aside and dusted his hands on each other. "They're too small to pump sewage or drinking water. Maybe they had a fluid electrical conductor of some sort. This building would then be a sort of amplifying relay station."

Licia and Auska peered down the opposite side of the road. "Look over there," Licia exclaimed.

"It's another building down there in the culvert," Tynan said. Only one of its walls was fairly intact. Several wide-diameter pipes ran through a relay inside the building. This ruin was thickly carpeted with snow-white flowers.

"Nagi," Auska said, "nagimo." Tabu.

Licia called to her, but Auska walked on to join her hunters.

"These look like flower trellises," Licia said, pointing to two troughs running along either side of the pipes.

"And here," Tynan said, stepping rapidly around the inside of the wall, "are smaller pipes running along the wall. They run through meters, it looks like. Look at the broken glass and the enameled dials. " Age-smoothed fragments of glass and ceramic crunched under his feet. "This was definitely a pumping station. But for what?"

Paul studied the array of green-stained white enamel dials. "Probably ran from Akha to Shka. Maybe on a whole network of old towns that are now nothing but primitive villages. But what were they pumping?"

"Look at these lamps," Licia said several feet away. Auska kept close to Licia, looking almost scared at this mystifying evidence of her people's past.

"Light bulbs?" Tynan, the engineer, seemed more alive than he had been in the weeks since their arrival. A row of what looked like broken light bulbs were spaced about three feet apart along the conduits. "Look, they have no filament inside. I think I have some idea what went through these pipes."

"What do you think?" Paul asked.

"Natural gas. See, they planted flowers because whenever a break appeared, the flowers would close up. The bulbs were for gas light—with the flames completely closed off from the pumping system. Each bulb had an intake and outlet for air."

"What about that other place across the road that Paul climbed down into?" Licia asked.

"I have a theory," Tynan said, climbing quickly back onto the road, followed by the others. "Information. Pure information."

"You've lost us."

"Communications, right? In our text books on Earth, we frequently used the analogy between electricity and water, right? To explain voltage. In an electrical conductor, electrons flow from an area of high concentration to one of low concentration once you complete the circuit. We would take sound; convert it to a code of moving electrons; at the other end we changed the electrical impulses back into sound. Suppose you were to use water in place of electrons? Water cannot be compressed—so you have a technology of hydraulics—vastly refined, of course, in ways I can't even guess at. If you want to use water to transmit a telephone conversation, you take the speaker's voice, which is air pressure; maybe you amplify it somehow with a system of drums and hammers; you change it to a code of pulses; pulse this pressure against a pipe of water of tiny diameter but ten, twenty, a hundred miles long; and convert the hydraulic pressure back into sound at the other end. Along the way, you could amplify or repeat the signal. You could use gas-driven engines to power the whole."

"Maybe that is why they put the two types of station so close to each other," Licia suggested.

They rejoined Auska, who waited for them anxiously while the hunters were already another few hundred feet ahead. "Nagimo, nagimo!" Auska whispered urgently, waving her arms forward.

Licia said: "They're anxious to get through the woods before dark."

Paul thought of the bellowing beast, whatever it was. "Can't blame them for that."

As they continued their journey, they encountered more combinations of these buildings, always on opposite sides of the road. In one place they found a ruined settlement that might have been a combination farm and station-keeper's house.

As they left the forest and walked in open veldt again, the hunters began to banter among each other again. Auska was learning a kind of pidgin English. She seemed to get along best with Licia. Paul was wary of Auska, not wanting to be conned into going native. Tynan showed her moments of kindness, but as they drew near Shka, he became increasingly morose.

They made camp under the stars. The hunters took turns standing guard. Paul and Licia sought each other's warmth. Auska slept in a simple blanket between the hunters and Paul and Licia. Tynan put his shelter up by himself, off to one side.

Soon after daybreak the next day, they came to the outskirts of Shka. Shielding his eyes, Paul counted not one but four mounds, all covered, surrounding the village. On one the natives had planted a vineyard. Except that Shka was larger and situated on slightly elevated ground, it was not much different from Akha. The similarity told Paul that there must once have been a homogeneous culture over much of N60A. Shka had a three-chimney kiln in its center. Two post roads crossed another in the center of the village. The kiln had been erected in the middle of what must once have been a sort of traffic circle for stone-wheeled wagons. "Imagine the traffic that must once have passed here," Licia said.

Tynan said: "My head wants to keep moving, but my feet are dragging. I want to get far from this place, but then again I just want to lie down here and die."

A group of men, women, and children came up to meet them just outside the village. The hunters waved their spears like big conquerors and enjoyed the attention. The natives peppered Auska with questions, glancing often at the odd visitors. Tynan told Paul: "No sign of Ongka's local equivalent. He bound up my leg and sent me to Akha. A younger fellow, but he also wears a shiny disk."

"Probably gone to Avamish," Paul said. "Ongka probably came through here."

Auska addressed a question about Ongka to an elderly woman whose sling bra hung flat against gray, wrinkled skin. The woman launched into a rapid explanation with gestures. Licia shook her head, having lost track of the conversation. Auska explained: "Ongka—here—one day—one night—say we come—gone to city."

Tynan side-mouthed to Paul: "I guess you were right. Ongka passed through here and picked up the local shaman on his way. Must be some to-do there in the old city."

"We eat," Auska said.

"Good old kiln," Tynan said. Surrounded by friendly people exactly like those in Akha, they ate their first hot meal since leaving the other village.

At that moment, Auska uttered a shriek. A young man holding a spear pushed against her shoulder with one hand and yelled at her. The hunters were by her side in a moment, separating her from a group of glaring young men. Paul and Tynan slowly moved their weapons around to the ready. Paul heard the catch of Licia's rifle slide quietly open.

The young man pranced demonstratively about, pointing to himself with the air of one who does not yet have authority but soon will. Auska and her hunters stood fast.

The local women backed away. It was the first time Paul had seen signs of fear in these people. "I wonder if these joes are from the same village," he muttered to Licia while trying to look neutral. Licia rose and stepped to Auska's side. She asked: "What's the matter?"

Auska gave her a troubled look. "He say Avamish nagimo—ngo back,"

The young man spread his arms and offered a last, sweeping word of disparagement, giving Paul and Licia bad looks, before stamping off accompanied by his followers.

Auska's hunters glared after the local boys. Auska seemed near tears but put up a brave front. The local women closed around her in a babble of apologies. "Young men," she told Licia and Paul, "much drink, much bestibo. Moliam bestibo."

"We won't stay in this village long," Paul said.

"For once, I agree right away," Licia said.

Soon, they finished their meal. Alone with Licia and Paul, Tynan said: "I have to pay her a visit." Paul didn't know what to say, and exchanged stymied looks with Licia. Tynan added: "You're welcome to come along."

Paul noticed the boisterous young men seemed to have disappeared. This surprised him, since he'd figured they'd trail the Earth people everywhere from here on in; he'd debated about warning them off with a shot. But the countryside all around appeared peaceful.

Auska and the hunters withdrew to the village chief's hut, where a group of women gathered protectively outside.

To get to the grave, Paul, Licia, and Tynan had to pass through the village's lush gardens. A great variety of fruits and vegetables were in various stages of ripeness. In the orchards, small kilns smoked, distilling wine, so that a fruity sweetness hung in the air. People worked here and there at a leisurely pace in the last days of harvest. An adolescent boy dropped his hoe and chased a pretty, shrieking young girl who had been picking berries in an adjacent garden.

They left the village and delved into rolling grasslands. They followed a hard-trodden path among scattered messy boulders. The four mounds fell behind away. They came to a small forest, and in the forest lay a swamp dotted with trees and patches of grass.

On the shore of a small lake, black with deposited pine needles, lay a cigar-shaped life ship, about 20 feet in diameter and 100 feet long. It was very similar to the one Paul and Licia had crashed in. The Aerie folk had cannibalized an abandoned CANUSAMEX space station to build the mother ship and its components for the 1000-year journey. None of the old UNASA rescue and reentry lifeboats was identical to any other, but they were of the same generic line. The boat lay on the edge of the lake, pointed into the water. It was hauntingly out of place both in its smooth texture and imposing size. The dark green silence in the wood made it all the more eerie. Its tall, lightly curving sides were scorched from a reentry, and gouged from a landing. It lay slightly tipped to one side and obviously would never fly again. The lower of its broad, stubby air foils was buried in spongy mud, while the opposite had been nearly severed and hung accordion-shaped down to the curve of the boat's underbelly. By now, only the tail protruded completely from the placid black lake water. Only the thick reeds underneath saved it from sinking faster. The broken cockpit windows were only about a foot above the water line by now.

Licia cried quietly as Tynan crouched over a mound of earth nearby on higher ground.

Paul climbed up into the lifeboat. Already, there were bird droppings on the seats inside the burned and shattered main area. Lizards fled as he dragged his feet through debris. He climbed over torn cushions and piles of shattered glass. Warped disks of Shakespeare, Newton, Caesar mixed with those of Einstein, Galileo, and everyone else ever brilliant on Earth—fused together in a slag heap that could never be undone—gone forever. Gone, Paul thought, like those in his own lifeboat and in the mother ship. That left only the Wengs—and where were they? Were they alive? With two out of three boats crashed, that did not bode well for the third boat—and the deadly radio silence all but shut the book.

Climbing out to rejoin the others, Paul read the legend on the ship's hull with bitter pride. The peeling letters said : EARTH.

The hulk slept silently on the haunted lake shore.

From the depths of the forest, from the darkest hidden places, from the underside of the planet, a siren-like predatory bellow sounded. It echoed a thousand times over the water. Something immense and lurking, Paul thought.

Tynan was just turning away from his spouse and companion's grave. His face was ashen with grief. His eyes looked wide and shocked. Licia stared at Paul with tear-beaded eyes and a grimace of a sob on her face.

Like forest spirits, a group of native men stood at the edge of the forest. They did not appear to be the same group of young toughs who had bothered them in the village—or were they? Seen from inside the forest, they looked luminous, almost enveloped in a kind of haze in the midday sun. They carried spears and shields. Each had painted a white stripe down his forehead. They looked menacing, but they didn't move. They didn't make a sound. *Just stared.*

26. New World—Year 3301

They spent the night at a quiet campsite far from the village, outside some ruins. The local toughs appeared to have given up their pursuit. The three protectors kept close to Auska, whom they were sworn to protect with their lives. The three young men kept eyeing the high grass to either side warily. Paul, Tynan, and Licia walked in a triangle formation behind their companions. All three held their rifles in firing position, trigger finger curled around the trigger cage, safety off, ready to start blasting. But no attack came. The high grass just sighed in the wind with memories of Avamish.

In this tension, Paul found Licia distant. Tynan, still hurting from Nancy's grave, kept to himself. Auska, as the day wore on and her protectors relaxed a bit, spent more time with Licia, learning the language, communicating in short conversations punctuated with laughter.

Toward dusk they finished what food they'd brought from Shka, cold. They did not want to advertise their location with a fire. Each kept to his or her own blankets. During Paul's turn at guard, he felt a chill up and down his back as something rooted in the ruins in the middle of the night. At the sound of a snort, he gripped his rifle harder and kept his back to a tree. There was a short cry, and the rooting animal must have gotten its prey, for there was a brief thrashing as it ran away and after that he only heard birds and insects.

The next morning, they were awakened by the voices of passing people. The natives carried amphorae of wine and stocks of food and seemed in high spirits. Their women wore long wrap-arounds, and hats resembling a small sunshade atop a turban. When the natives saw the Earth people, they stopped to stare, to point, to make unfriendly remarks. Five or six dark-skinned men challenged Paul and Tynan.

Auska and her three protectors stepped out and faced down the challenge. Paul was impressed. Auska carried an aura of authority and impatience, mirroring Ongka's. The natives' demeanor softened somewhat. They spoke briefly with her, jabbered with her hunters, were not unfriendly. Paul and Tynan kept their weapons ready. Licia hadn't had time to grab her rifle, but she sat by her shelter holding her handgun, which looked huge and dull and black; each shot would lay out one or more adults foolish enough to challenge her.

The natives abruptly turned and started back on their journey, arguing among each other who was to carry what, and which jug should be opened next.

Paul breathed a sigh of relief when the natives went on their way. A few uncomplimentary comments drifted back toward the humans. "They were carrying lots of wine," Licia said. "They were nasty-loopy."

"Mnasty-mgloopy," Auska said with humor in her anger. "We go now city."

On their journey, they met with several more groups. Most of the natives treated them with civility and otherwise ignored them. Only one or two other groups seemed hostile. "Depends on how much they've been drinking," Tynan remarked.

They passed more ruined way stations, which by now weren't so exciting anymore. They all looked very much alike. Moreover, the sense of foreboding, of hidden danger, grew as they neared Avamish, and diminished their scientific curiosity.

Once, Paul pointed to the horizon. There he saw, again, a single file of warriors. They carried spears and shields, and each in turn looked toward the humans. They did not stop or slow down, but were clearly hurrying toward the great city. Their heads looked dark in profile. The sight of the white paint when they turned to face him chilled Paul. The silence of those penetrating looks seemed predatory.

Finally, during their fifth or sixth day on the post road, a change came.

"Did you hear something?" Licia suddenly asked.

"Sounds like thunder far away," Tynan said. Paul, straining his ears, heard it too.

Auska and her guardians walked slightly ahead. Slim, majestic figures, they now walked more apprehensively. Their footsteps were measured and careful. Their banter had quieted, and they shared few smiles among each other.

Paul heard a sound like distant, constantly growling thunder— at odds with the peacefulness of the blue sky. He listened intently, trying to figure out what caused the noise. There was little to glean

from the steady, throaty growl. "Reminds me of Earth," he said after
a while.

"Thunder," Tynan agreed.

Licia said nothing. They all remembered well the constant
growl of thunder in the heavy black clouds that covered the Earth's
surface, and grew higher every year.

27. Old World—Year 2299

Paul was twenty-three. As he hurried through the silent Aerie corridors, he glanced idly through its windows at the passing sunny fields of snow. His heart pounded, for he wanted so badly to be in engineering, and he was afraid he would be stymied again. Three years ago, the Council had pegged him as a generalist constable, and he'd lost three precious research years.

Thunder constantly shook the Aerie. Technicians never ceased combing the hive city for dangerous fissures in its walls.

Paul entered the library in search of Dr. SheuXe. He queried the librarian, an elderly man amid a world of books and carpets and musty smells. "Dr. SheuXe is in Reading Room 607," was the whispered prompt.

Paul found his mentor in a blind little room filled with gray, fossil volumes that recalled Earth's civilization. "You sent for me, Sir?"

Dr. SheuXe looked up, his eyes glazed from reading. His white hair looked rumpled as if he had often run his hands through it in perplexity. "Oh, Paul, Paul, how is my student today?"

"I am fine, Sir. I finished my constabulary ten days ago and I am anxiously awaiting the next stage of my education."

"Quite so," SheuXe said. "I have been reading about lost civilizations."

"You mean like Rome and New York?" He wondered what this might have to do with his life's occupation.

"Not exactly, Paul. I have been reading ancient imaginative literature, stories of what might have been."

"Those old rocket stories?"

"Yes. Old stories. Tales of what might have been, were it not for the clouds and the Earth's—OUR Earth's dying." The old man sighed. "Oh, Paul." His eyes filled with distance. "It could have been a glorious future, this today of ours."

"Sir, about my own future."

SheuXe snapped back to the present. "Yes!" He pointed to a chair. "Sit down, my boy. Do you know it's been over three centuries since humans went into space?"

Paul felt a rush of interest and apprehension—the first, for the smell of adventure; the second, for fear that it was a false alarm. Yes, man had gone into space, colonized the Moon, Mars, the Lagrange Points. Man had begun to build habitats even further out, had readied ships to explore the nearer stars. Then the series of natural disasters had struck, and Earth civilization had imploded on itself. The last colonies in space had been abandoned a century ago.

"There are empty space stations up there, Paul. Ships. Lifeboats. Lots of hardware. Some of it's been sieved by micro-meteorites. Most of it's simply in cold storage up there, beautifully preserved. We are already getting teams ready to start putting together what's salvageable."

"I would love to be part of that," Paul said.

SheuXe smiled mysteriously. "It will become much, much more interesting." As he spoke, the clouds below slammed with long fusillades of thunder. "And not a day too soon."

28. New World—Year 3301

The sound of thunder grew near as they walked along the ancient post road.

Licia saw it first. "The sea!"

They were on high ground. Around them in all directions stretched grassland, with an occasional clump of stone or ruins. Far away, off to their right, just below the horizon, gleamed a mirror surface reflecting the pink-gold sun above.

Their path, however, was taking them past the sea, down into a lower region that disappeared into mist. The thundering grew deeper and closer as they walked. The sunlight faded away, and an eternal foggy dampness enveloped them in unreality. They sniffed curiously at the gray, wet sky. A disturbed wind combed through the bowed grass.

A cry of "nagimo!" came from Auska's companions. At first they balked at approaching Avamish. Then the sight of other natives passing shamed them into a wary silence. Now Paul, Licia, and Tynan walked ahead while Auska and the hunters trailed.

They passed an encampment on a plain that was bisected by the post road. Native people cooked over a small kiln of gathered rocks, while others rested under a blanket spread under trees. They took little notice of the pioneers. In an nearby field, some eight or ten men hunted. The men stalked much as the native dogs did, but with spears raised for deadly throwing.

The prey showed itself: a wild swine, massive and low-built, with the same powerful rear haunches as most of the planet's animals. Twin ridges of stiff bristles ran along the animal's spine in an otherwise smooth back. Its snout, bristling with hook-shaped teeth, dripped with saliva as it charged the baiting scouts. It made a steady roaring sound, almost like a motor, in its anger. And it came right at Paul and Licia.

The hunters surrounded Auska, spears held high to kill the animal, but it ran far around them.

Licia screamed. Tynan and Paul whirled simultaneously to watch the pig's mate gallop across the post road to protect his female. Standing four feet at the shoulder, the boar was an overwhelming spectacle as it charged past Paul at 10 feet. Paul saw enraged little red eyes and a slavering, tremulous snout issuing gouts of saliva and steam. The animal's insane fury made Paul quake. He felt cold sweat as he put his arm around Licia.

The encamped hunters moved smoothly in concert. They held a net in the air. The boar took the knotted twine without wavering in his charge. The ground shook—but more from the distantly visible edge of the shimmering sea.

The hunters moved agilely as if in a dance. The boar pounded among them, unable to break his charge. Clubs broke the boar's weaker forelegs and he thrashed down in a shower of dirt and grass. Instantly the hunters were upon him, goring with their spears.

They brought the sow down in a similar flurry of stone spears. The women cheered by the road while the men waved their weapons in triumph. Paul suddenly realized he'd been gripping his rifle tensely, and now he let it slip by his side. He felt dazed by the roar of the sea and the pounding passage of the now-dead animal.

They left the hunting scene behind as they descended into the mist. Gradually the landscape changed. Fog hung darkly around them, brushing their faces with tiny raindrops. Their arms and faces dripped with dampness. The surrounding trees and hills looked ghostly. Auska and the hunters trudged behind them like silent ghosts.

At last they came upon the source of the noise.

Paul suddenly remembered the planet's geology as seen from space. The continent was split by a fault up to a mile wide in places. A deafening chaos of water poured from a hundred mighty rivers on the continent's surface, spewing through the fault and out into the sea.

Baked in the sun's occluded heat, dozens of rainbows shimmered above the bone-white walls of the fault, which at this point was about 1,000 feet wide.

Clinging to the walls inside the fault were ancient ruins, piled one upon the other and stuck to the thousand foot high walls in a mass so dense it seemed they must all fall down into the thundering gorge in another second. The gouged, blind remains seemed dazed by light and noise. Tynan's mouth moved wetly and vainly, for his voice was drowned out but his meaning was clear: these must be the main power stations of the vanished Senders.

The noise was painful to hear. Water dripped from their faces, making them blink and sputter. A single-span stone bridge miraculously arched the chasm, placed there centuries ago. Against the walls of the fault, ten foot wide cylindrical ducts hung down broken off near the water line. The water was hypnotic to look at. It raced down-continent, in waves dozens of feet high, flying with speed, intersecting and crossing each other, in places green as bottle glass, in places amber, in places marbled with white foam, in places white as milk, all running together in a mesmerizing display. No sooner did Paul fasten his eyes upon a point, then that point had moved a hundred feet. He learned to spot objects—fallen trees, bushes, even a drowned buffalo—bobbing past at a good clip a thousand feet below.

The post road ran right up to the bridge and stopped. The bridge was about twenty feet across and appeared to be made of a light, almost translucent gray stone. It looked like soapstone, but Paul bet it was tough as steel. On either edge of the bridge, it rose up about three feet in a low protective wall.

Clinging together in two groups—Paul's and Auska's—they crossed the bridge. Like a thread, the bridge spanned a mile of raging water. The bridge trembled constantly under the assault of noise alone.

Suddenly Licia pointed out to sea with her free hand. Her eyes were wide and her mouth moved soundlessly.

About a mile or two out in the briny ocean, a pair of gray shapes thrashed about in the foaming, mountainous waves.

Paul could not tell what the shapes were. They reminded him of the extinct Earth whale, only several times larger.

One creature, large as a zeppelin, reared out of the water, propelled by immense tail and flippers. First its bluntly rounded head projected above the waves to a height of fifty feet. Then the head fell back into the water. The rest of the body, a tapered ship of muscle and bone a hundred feet long, followed the head back under water, leaving a huge splash. Paul remembered the gigantism of the turtles they had passed, and the howlings from the forests which had first impressed them. N60A must have undreamed secrets under its usually placid surface.

After this brilliant leap through the air, the post road continued on again, arrow-straight.

Rows of badly ruined buildings, reminding Paul of abandoned factories, lined this rim of the gorge, as well as both sides of the post road. The area was well-overgrown with trees, and in the trees everywhere were the shells of abandoned houses.

"Suburbs," Paul said when he could be heard.

Tynan was excited again. "Just a look, Menard. This must have been a tremendous power-generating plant for the whole city. Probably fed the hydraulic communication system for their whole civilization." Tynan clambered off to one side and up a mound of rubble. Paul followed. Auska seemed terrified of the city and its ghosts, and remained stubbornly planted on the road. Licia stayed with her.

One building was three stories high and several hundred feet long. Its rear overhung the gorge. Great pipes—the ones they'd seen from the opposite rim—extended down to the water line. Inside, the building was a roofless rubble of stone and mud overgrown with greenery.

Auska and her companions walked several hundred feet ahead, as they had done in the forest before Shka, evidently to distance themselves from this disrespect to the ghosts of Avamish.

Beside the building was a tower shaped structure a hundred feet high. Paul felt awed, dwarfed by the massive scale of the ancients' architecture. An aqueduct led toward the fabled city, which could not be far now that they stood in its exurbs.

When Paul returned to the road, Licia said, wrinkling her nose, "I smell something. Gas, I think." They traced the odor to slightly higher ground on the landward side. Past a dense thicket of woods, they found a park-like area of sparse trees. Ragged streams of frozen, crumbling lava had become overgrown with grass. All around were low domes of stone. A few oozed thin tendrils of acrid white smoke. Huge stone machines and kilns surrounded the periphery.

"Look on the ground," Licia said.

Everywhere lay pieces of tools—handles, hammer heads, halves of pliers. "It's a foundry," Tynan exclaimed. "Of course! Think of it. On Earth, the stone age naturally gave way to successive ages of metals. Even on Earth, stone age man had some high moments, if you remember Stonehenge. There were Neolithic quarries where our ancestors dug out good rocks and manufactured tools for trading across huge distances. Yes, and think of New York City. On Earth, the stone age continued parallel to the ages of metals and nuclear energy. Stone is a vital tool that man could not abandon. Here, there are no metals, so they took the stone age to its ultimate expression. They used volcanic furnaces to smelt the most complex alloys of stone you can imagine. Think of the temperatures it takes to melt stone!"

Licia cried out from beyond some trees: "I think I may have found the Senders' equipment. Over here."

They found her at the edge of what looked like a stone amphitheater. At the bottom of the depression was a sort of blockhouse.

"I think you're right, Lish," Tynan said. He knelt to examine some of the cylindrical stone blocks rising like seats all around. "Look, Menard, there are rust stains everywhere. At one time, this whole depression was covered with a lacework of metal. Sure, it makes sense. They took what little metal they had and built a radio dish next to their power source. What power that water must generate!"

Paul stared down at the blockhouse. If Tynan and Licia were right, long ago that squat, ugly structure must have bustled with technicians and scientists. He remembered the day Gregory died, the day the signals were first received. The amphitheater had a melancholy atmosphere. The blockhouse reminded him of pictures he'd seen of the abandoned temples of Yucatan. In the lush silence, many questions hung over the darkly yawning, lizard-infested building.

When they joined Auska, her eyes were wide with wonder at the achievements of her forebears—if indeed the villagers were of the same race. Auska had overcome her timidity somewhat and poked around in some ruined houses that might once have had pleasant yards, verandahs, and gardens. Her companions hung back in a sullen trio.

"No signs of war." Paul remembered the skulls in the mound at Akha, and wasn't sure. "Everything seems to have been left lying all of a sudden. Why? What did they look like? Where did they go?"

An hour or two passed as they walked along the road. They passed several major crossroads. Everywhere were empty houses. Bright green trees reared up wild on either side of the road.

Everywhere was a spell of enchantment. Paul thought back to pictures he'd seen of American suburbs in the late 20th century. In one place they found what looked like a playground full of children's crawl-through toys. He thought of other pictures—of the ruins of Pompeii, of Rome after its long and terrible death.

Auska skimmed along the edge of the road, picking flowers that she gave to each of her companions, perhaps as a charm against the ghosts lurking in the villas all around. Licia passed a canteen of water around. They ate heartily the last of their canned rations atop a hill from which they could see for miles around. Above the far tree crowns loomed broken spires, truncated towers, and the blunted tips of crumbling pyramids. "That's got to be the city itself," Paul said, wondering if that were true, or if it went on like this for many miles, building to some great climax. "We've got to get into the soul of it, find out what makes it tick."

Tynan looked sullen. "You haven't tasted death here like I have. I think it's all a big flower, just waiting for us to nuzzle close before it slams shut and devours us."

"We should be careful," Licia seconded. She gave Paul a glaring look.

Wounded, Paul left the other three to rest in the shade. Making a small excursion through the ruins, he came upon a recessed area surrounded by a stone wall. Within were several pyramids and temple-like structures with neither doors nor windows. Puzzled, he walked around several of these structures, until he came to a blind doorway. Hewn directly into the white marble was the imitation of a doorway. On either side of the doorway was a flat continuous surface depicting a scene in low relief. It was the first bit of art work he'd had found on N60A. He forgot his anger and ran back to call Licia. Tynan came instead.

"It is sublime," Tynan allowed. They stood back.

"This is a tomb, I think."

"I think so," Tynan whispered.

"Well now we know. There they are, the Senders. That's what they looked like."

The scene showed a man and a woman sitting on stools facing each other. The figures had all the physical attributes of Ongka's people, including the way their hair grew. The scene glowed with simple, studied clarity, and it matched the finest artistic achievements of lost Earth.

The man and the woman toasted each other with goblets. The man had a thin, carefully manicured beard and was naked from the waist up save a pair of broad belts that crossed in the middle of his chest and extended over the shoulders. He was bald on top, but had a gently understated mane of hair over each shoulder. He was powerful and muscular-looking, but in good, modest proportion. Around his waist was a thick, corded belt, from which a loose dress extended down to his mid-calves. His feet were shod in heavy leather sandals, Roman-style. His face was elegant and sophisticated; the smiling, small mouth and narrow almond eyes were directed over the rim of his goblet at the woman opposite. The look they exchanged was filled with lively humor and urbanity, which Paul remembered from artwork left by Cretan and Middle Eastern people of ages ago.

The woman—or girl—was smaller than the man. Like Auska, she had a shock of (he assumed) silvery hair like a close-cropped helmet. Her feet were bare. She wore a long, single-piece gown or chlamys draped over one shoulder, looped down across her belly and back, to join into a single piece extending to mid-calf. Her delicate, small feet and exquisitely tapered lower legs were exposed. The stool she sat on might have been a bit too large for her, because her legs were tucked slightly under it, crossed at the ankles, toes touching the floor, while the man's feet rested flat, one slightly ahead of the other. The girl's chlamys left exposed the shoulder facing Paul, which tapered into a small soft arm. Also exposed was the side of her torso, which was long and girlish like Auska's, pert and round in the waist and buttock, and she revealed one small spherical breast set high like Auska's, with the nipple indicated as a faintly raised circle with a pucker in the middle. Her left hand, closer to·Paul, was relaxed and curled in her lap. The right arm raised a glass to the man's. Her face shimmered with a demure yet somehow mysteriously sensuous, delighted guile.

Their eyes looked directly into one another's. Paul wondered about the equation, the infinite geometry, of this gaze. How many centuries had that gaze of obvious nuptial love remained interlocked unmindful of the deterioration of their forest-drowned world?

"There they are, the Senders," Tynan said quietly as Licia and Auska quietly joined them. Wonderingly, Auska drew a finger lightly along the man's beautiful face. Tynan added: "Spoused, you can bet."

"Husband and wife," Licia said with certainty, stressing this world's cultural ways.

"They are buried in there," Paul said with certainty.

Tynan looked closer. "Look at the detail. It's incredible. There are flowers and grass along the lower edge of the frieze. And look at that bower of leaves and twigs and berries curving around the top. Every detail shows. And look deeper. You can see the city, the whole city, as it once was."

Behind the couple, in the far distance, Paul saw sky-scraping buildings and an expanse of sky. The buildings looked elfin— interconnected with high-flung ramps and arching bridges. The bridges, like that spanning the gorge, were of an art different from any achieved on Earth. Also unlike Earth's great buildings of the late period, these were not blunt rectangles of metal and glass, but they flowered in a profusion of all the universal geometric shapes.

Then Licia made a discovery within the frieze. In a small area, between some rooftops near the center of the city, was a mess of detail so fine it looked as though it had been carved in glass, and its smallest components seemed to lose themselves into the very pores of the stone.

"Clouds," Paul interpolated.

"Smoke," Tynan thought. "Do you see a shape in it though?"

They all stared closely. Licia said: "It's pretty well hidden in the smoke, if smoke it is. Looks like an egg, or a dome."

"Look next to it," Tynan said.

Paul exclaimed: "Lord, you're right. It's a rocket lifting off from a launch pad!"

"No," Licia said. Then she staggered back a step. "So they did master space flight?"

Within minutes, they found other reliefs.

Plainly visible was a scene depicting an elderly couple. An old man in a long robe held a stick with which he playfully goaded a small furry animal resembling a cat. The woman sat nearby on a stool. She watched the domestic scene with stately serenity. Her hands were interlocked in the folds of her robe. The couple were in a garden. Perhaps this was an older tomb, for the city skyline looked sparser and there were no rockets in evidence. Tynan suggested: "We could probably date the tombs by comparing skylines."

Thousands of tombs covered the adjoining area. They were in a vast necropolis.

Auska's eyes shone pleasurably in this great place of her ancestors. Paul supposed she also looked forward to seeing her uncle soon.

As they walked on, everywhere amber and green light played on ruins under trees. The late summer heat pressed, and they grew tired. Paul felt again that melancholy something that reached right into his soul and tugged painfully at the fiber of his being. He remembered Ongka, the clockwork, the probing of his mind. It seemed almost as though the city had telepathic waves about it, as if it had a soul of its own.

The many windows of deserted dwellings gazed after the travelers with gloomy eye sockets. The forest was lively but haunted. Bees with great butterfly wings droned unmindfully in search of flower prey.

Stopping to rest, they were surprised by a band of natives carrying amphorae. Paul and Licia had their sidearms ready. Tynan slowly undid his rifle strap. The natives had been drinking and were in an ugly mood. As they passed, they waved spears and made unsavory remarks. Once again, Auska stepped forth, frail wiry figure protecting her alien companions. This time, her companions were ready for a fight. They appeared to be in a vile mood, afraid of the ghosts in the city, resentful of the alien pioneers who had forced them here. The standoff with the passing natives was brief. Auska resolved it peaceably as she explained something to them. For some reason, the Earth people were important. The villagers backed off suspiciously and marched on.

Slowly, Paul returned his weapon to safety. The three hunters commandeered the road ahead. Auska followed them. Paul, Licia, and Tynan walked behind. "What are you getting us into, Menard?" Tynan grumbled in a low voice. Licia seconded: "Paul, I don't know if we should be doing this. It feels so—out of control."

Paul considered. Had he made a mistake? Perhaps. They had to know about the city. They had to stick together. Hence, they had come here. But he'd exposed them to the danger of a fatal run-in with armed and drunken natives. For the first time, he felt a chill of morbid apprehension that he might be utterly wrong. And that the remnants of Earth's expedition would pay for it.

"No answer?" Tynan goaded.

"We'll see," Paul said curtly.

Tynan rolled his eyes up. Licia looked furious.

Suddenly, every echo among the tree trunks spelled ambush. More than once, they stood stock still, overcome by the haunted forest of ruins. Every grave seemed to emanate a soul wanting to communicate. Desperately. Fearfully. Paul sensed some terrible trouble impending the closer they came to the city. They would not tread lightly and innocently among its mysteries, he knew. He saw the same thoughts reflected in Tynan's and Licia's eyes. He saw other things there too, that troubled him deeply.

29. New World—Year 3301

The city, when they came to it that afternoon, was a staggering sight.

Avamish was colossal and beautiful, even in death. It lay in a gently sloping bowl of earth about five miles across and a thousand feet deep. Millions of people might once have lived here. There were thousands of buildings, some towering as high as the bowl's rim.

Auska and the hunters got there first. They stood on the rim looking down into the city, like figures in a magnificent diorama. For the first time, the young men laughed and pointed excitedly.

Paul felt dazed. Licia and Tynan all seemed moody. The late afternoon air had a haze that settled mightily among the trees and ruins. There was a faintly smoky smell. Maze upon maze of buildings poured out of the city, overwhelming its suburbs, and spreading for miles beyond.

Post roads from all over the planet converged on Avamish. In the center of the city were the most fantastic and sprawling structures of all—which could only be the remains of an abandoned star port. The road they had been traveling led down into the city, joined by dozens of local feeder roads.

Auska's companions pointed off to the left, on the gentle slopes leading down into the city. Now Paul understood the smoky smell. Spread over a plateau, overlooking the city, were a thousand or more tents. Auska gestured for them to follow her. "Ongka hada. Moniam bestibo."

The distant tent city bustled with foot traffic. In one place, dozens of people clambered around the carcass of a dead giant turtle. Makeshift kilns smoked with roasting turtle meat. Auska led them away from the tents, her form lithe and self-assured. No doubt she would be happy to see her uncle.

Paul did not immediately sense the sudden buildup of tension among Auska's group as they passed through a grassy, sunny clearing abuzz with insects. He felt lulled by the smell of food, by the quiet. Already the sun reddened within the city haze, and darkness forked through the tree crowns.

Suddenly, something hit Paul in the face. The pain was dulled only by the near-unconsciousness in which he found himself on the ground. Groggy, he tried to rise up on one elbow. He heard shouting—Auska's, Tynan's, Licia's. He heard other men's voices. Natives. Angry. As his vision returned, he glimpsed the rock that had hit him, the man with the ax upraised to kill him, and the scuffle in which Licia was thrown to the ground. He saw Tynan fingering his rifle, ready to shoot.

Auska stood protected by her companions. Her horrified eyes stared from among their grim faces. They made no move to help Paul or Licia.

The man holding the ax looked down with crazed eyes. He was one of the figures who bore a wide white stripe up his forehead and over the top of the head. The obsidian blade glinted with a coppery sheen—looking death in the face, Paul clearly made out the greenish-black gleam of the rock, and the bloody redness of the sun reflected within it.

Then, before anyone could move, a voice arose from somewhere. A young man's voice. "Nagi! Nagi! Nasso mnalaminam bindi!" There was authority in that adolescent voice. And something familiar.

The ax wielder's hate-filled eyes wavered. Uncertainty flickered, and he staggered back a step, lowering the ax out of striking pose. Licia, propped on one elbow, quietly extracted her handgun, ready to shoot. Paul held up his hand, signaling Licia and Tynan to hold fire. Auska rushed to Paul's side, offering a cloth to wipe blood from his cheek. The rock had come out of nowhere and split the skin on his cheekbone.

"Nagi!" the voice said again, "no!" Paul stared as a tall young man entered the clearing. He also had a stripe painted on his forehead and was followed by other men of all ages with a similar decoration.

"Amda!" Paul exclaimed. Behind the boy was his chunkier companion, Dunda. Same white face. Neither smiled. On Amda's chest glittered a brand-new copper disk. Amda issued orders, and the stripemen withdrew. He spoke sharply to Auska, who acted deferentially. "Po-wul," he said, "Li-sha." He waved his hand for them to stay away from the tents. "Tay-non." He pointed down into the city and shrugged. Then he pointed to Paul. Finally he pointed to the four points of the compass, but ordered them to stay away from the tent city.

"Auska," Amda said, "nagi mPowul mLisha..." He poured a torrent of instructions, each time cutting off her objections. Her three companions braggingly joined the ranks of the stripemen, as if relieved of some unwanted burden. Amda shouted at his cousin: "Apatimo h'Ongka!" That was the final word. With a pained look back at her pioneer companions, she followed Amda when he turned and walked off. The rest of the natives followed.

Paul, Licia, and Tynan were alone in the clearing.

"Let's get out of here," Tynan said. "Let's get the hell back to Akha."

They trudged away, not wanting to go into the unknown of the City as dusk came, but back up to safety beyond the rim. Stars already twinkled in the bleach-blue sky. Auska began sobbing quietly to herself, trying to hide her feelings behind her hands. Licia told Paul sharply: "I knew this trip was a mistake. I knew it all along."

"We'll be lucky if we get out of this area alive," Tynan said.

Paul held a rag to his swollen, throbbing cheek and felt uncertain. Maybe they were right. Maybe the survive/conquer instruction was all wrong. Maybe it should be survive/stay out of the way. All he could say was: "It's getting dark. We should really stop here."

Tynan looked around sarcastically. "What, camp on the road?"

"I'm not going anywhere down there," Licia said, shivering. Paul followed her gaze to the sunken houses on either side of the road. Under the bushes that grew on their walls, the insides were no doubt filled with water and things that crawled through mud.

"Over there," Paul said. He pointed to an elevated room of some sort. Looked as though it had once been the upper story of a house. A thousand years of drifting dust had deposited a layer that had turned to soil and sprouted grass. They climbed up cautiously and explored. They were too tired to go any further. As darkness fell, Paul watched Licia drop her things on the ground and unpack her shelter and sleeping bag. Her gaze never met his, and her lips were pressed in a hard line. Paul unfolded his own shelter and bag on the dry, grassy soil. Tynan silently camped a few yards away. Then Licia screamed. Something—an orange lizard the size of

Paul's foot—darted through the grass and down into the street. "Paul, you are a fool," Licia wailed, "and I was a bigger fool for ever coming here with you!"

Paul wasn't sure if she meant Avamish, or the entire journey away from Earth. He lay awake, staring at the stars. Tynan began to snore. Licia sobbed steadily, and Paul crawled close to her to offer whispers of comfort. She pushed him roughly away. He looked at the stars and thought that maybe he should not have come here. He'd be long dead now, and so would Licia. Nothing more to worry about. Licia's sobbing got quiet, and pretty soon Paul was startled that his own snoring woke him. He stood up and looked around for any signs of danger. The city glittered in the light of the twin moons. Avamish almost looked as if it were still fully inhabited. Only the utter lack of city lights gave away that it was a dead place. To witness a death so big was unexpected and overpowering and depressing; more than the soul could bear. The Milky Way as always looked alien and slightly distorted from this vantage point. A cool wind, with foreign tenderness, bled through sifting leaves. Paul lay down. He listened for a moment—just night sounds, nothing extraordinary—and he turned onto his side, curled his arms around himself, and went back to sleep.

30. New World—Year 3301

Then it was dawn. Noise from the encampment drifted up to waken Paul. He sat up shivering and still tired; hungry. His body ached from hard spots he had not noticed before going to sleep. Tynan mixed dry rations with runoff dew from a small shelter trap. He used the last of the emergency cubes to heat the mixture. It was only lukewarm at that, and tasted like pea soup with something metallic in it. As they ate, they stared toward the city, which was hidden in fog. Avamish weighed greatly upon each of them. Tynan's face had that haunted look, that stare as if he were once more looking into Nancy's grave. Licia was not speaking to Paul.

Conquest, something reminded Paul. He almost had to laugh, were their situation here not so precarious. He remembered SheuXe's weary, intelligent face. Ongka's also drifted through his thoughts, amid that somber and grinding clockwork.

A thick fog veiled the immensity of Avamish.

"Hello," Paul said to Licia.

She gave him a look that said, you brought us here, now what? She looked down and moved a twig around with her finger.

Tynan said: "I must have sprained my ankle again, Or else it's this damp cold that gets into everything."

Paul saw that Tynan's ankle did look swollen. "All that walking."

"I suppose that means we're stuck here until it heals," Licia said.

The fog created a sense of oppression.

Paul said: "I bet we would find Ongka over there in that camp."

Licia said: "And not live to tell the tale."

Paul looked into her eyes. "I'm sorry you're unhappy." She didn't answer. Paul added: "The sun will soon come up and the fog will clear and everything will look different."

"Paul, we shouldn't be here. We should be back in our village."

"Didn't Ongka let us dig out the mound? Didn't he send Auska to guide us here?"

"He's alien, and we don't know what's in his mind."

"You're wrong. This world is our home now. We have a right to probe into every corner."

"You're crazy."

"You're frustrated."

"Frustrated. You're right."

Tynan worked hard to get his boot off. "Stop it, you two. If I could, I'd be down there exploring that city right now. Dammit." The boot came off. His ankle was swollen and purple.

Paul sighed with frustration. He picked up his rifle and canteen. "I'm going to take a walk down there. You stay here. Stay together, you hear?" They did not answer.

Paul wanted to get away, to walk, to move, anything but stay here and soak up this abuse from her. She might have a point, but she could be so bitchy and unforgiving. It was part of the Aerie way. There was never any room for error. You followed leaders blindly, and expected them to be right. He wasn't sure now that coming here at festival time might have been a great mistake. The kind for which Aerie leaders could be executed.

Rifle in hand, he picked his way down the Avamishan hillside along the ancient post road.

He felt himself being absorbed into the jumble of buildings on either side, and he welcomed the feeling. Fog yawned out of the unseeing eyes, the windows and doorways, of the city that was now theirs too. Their world, their heritage, to be explored and set aright. She'd come around to his point of view.

31. New World—Year 3301

As Paul delved into the city, the fog began to lift. N60, a watery yellow disk, poked warmly through the mist. He saw reliefs on the walls. In more than one building, old fountains still plashed under the natural pressure from the miles-distant gorge that had given the city energy, water, life. He saw pictures of space ports and of crowds of people milling about pointing to departing rockets.

A broken wagon lay shattered on a curb stone. A sharp-faced animal with a bushy blue-black tail and fat short legs darted from beneath the wagon and stared at Paul. He shot it. For a moment he thought about bringing it back to their camp. But he very deliberately cut pieces of its soft, bloody belly. He gathered dry brush and made a small fire. The meat seemed to cook well if you held it just close enough to the fire.

The fog turned thin and got yellowish. Balmy daylight was coming through. Soon his eyes penetrated to the still faraway center of the city. To the star port. At times, he thought he recognized the skyline from the tomb reliefs they had seen. The very shape and feel of the city mirrored some of the most basic and exalted human drives. Upward, it said. Where had he seen that before? Pictures of New York, before the clouds. Same slim, star-scraping buildings reaching up grandly, desperately, for immortality.

He felt the sense of mighty, unresolvable conflict between gravity and flight; between the defiantly gathered man-made buildings and the overpowering forces of nature all around laying siege. Avamish, like New York, was ancient as Ur of the Chaldees, modern as today. Avamish lived on, though its descendants had forgotten use of the wheel. Avamish was sublime.

On the rubble-strewn avenues he searched for the one landmark that was important to him: The star port dome depicted on the grave of the raised goblets. He stayed on the main roads, avoiding cul-de-sacs in which weeds and flowers choked up the windows and doorways. Paul had never been in a city, but he knew certain things to look for: hotels, police and fire stations, libraries, power plants, administrative buildings, schools.

On some of the larger surviving outside walls of large buildings, Paul saw huge figures in tiled relief. They were oddly different from people he'd seen here so far. Their skin coloring, as depicted on the twenty foot high reliefs, was redder. Their hair was different—that was it! The men were bearded; he had yet to see any hint of facial hair among these people. Had the rulers of Avamish been different? Paul remembered the skulls in the mound at Akha, with their shattered faces and bashed in eye sockets, and shuddered.

He found the space port in the center of the city. It covered several square miles. The launch pads themselves were in the exact center of the city and they had turned into wild gardens. Surrounding the launch pads to the east and seat were fantastically shaped buildings. Paul's spirit soared when he saw the rusted, crumbling framework atop one of the buildings. That had to be the telemetry center. Some buildings had turned into mounds of rubble. Everywhere were the bitten-off ends of conduit of all sizes, converging on the star port. No space craft of any recognizable description were evident. It would take time to explore this whole place; God was it huge! A lot of buildings appeared to be still intact. Using his flashlight to poke through a watery corridor, he forced a massive door off its crumbling stone hinges. Between windowless walls, he found the rusty remains of tons of sending and receiving equipment. Tynan would have a field day in here. Paul emerged into bright, hot morning sunshine. Far off on the hillsides, fog dissipated its last tendrils. Ghostly buildings lingered over treetops for miles around.

Paul walked along the outer perimeter of the launch area, on an elevated road of cracked concrete. Below him on the right were the remains of launch gantries. On the left were buildings, in fantastic shapes—some delicate, some ponderous. Concrete looped around concrete in pillars and circles.

Paul climbed through the broken shell of one diamond shaped building that might have been a hotel because it contained a multitude of small cubicles, each with its own bath. He found no evidence of electric outlets—but he did find speakers on the walls as well as smashed bell-ended handles on boxes, suggesting telephones. How ingeniously they must have engineered their hydraulic society!

The hotel, like most of the other buildings, had windows of all sizes and shapes: squares, circles, rectangles, rhombi, stars, arrows, human figures. In this, as in so many small touches, the Senders had been different from·humans. Earth people for no apparent reason made most windows into rectangles, except in churches, the most exalted human places. The effect of Avamish was not gaudy. Every detail occupied an understandable place. The effect was uplifting. It was free, undisciplined, pleasant. Still, there was something alien and disconcerting about it. Paul longed to figure out what that was. He felt sure that he would, if he poked around here long enough, and that when he understood it, he would understand much more about Avamish.

He found a large swimming pool half full of brackish water and populated by bright lizards—some orange and white spiral-covered, others green-striped and blue-diamond-backed—that treaded water and hissed at his appearance. Their eyes were burgundy, or was that hate?

He hurried past more stone shapes and tangles. Circles were everywhere—totems of the planet, emblems of the sun. Some buildings seemed to stand on their fingers like dancers, their fingertips balanced on the surfaces of reflecting pools while their bodies writhed in complex motions and nonmotions. Nothing stood still, everything stood still. Alien.

In counterpoint, some buildings were bottom-heavy Buddhas sitting on stumpy dolmen-like legs, in the midst of arrows flying through hoops and stochastically arranged stalagmites and stalactites of sugary marble. Conquest.

32. New World—Year 3301

Leaving the spaceport, Paul started back to camp by a slightly different route. He picked his way through the jumbled city blocks toward a broken dome, and as he drew near, he exclaimed. It was the dome they had seen in the tomb fresco. In his excitement, he nearly stepped off the edge of a flat concrete area. He looked down into a thousand-foot yawning depth filled with water. Shadows of buried machinery rippled between splashes of sunlight and the wakes of jetting squid. He staggered back dizzily. Birds wheeled shrieking over his head, and he recoiled with Aerie-bred fear of avians. Just under the water lay the bulk of a rocket body three times as large as the mother ship had been. The rocket's thin, alloy-tough skin looked broken; a shark sized fish with twin catamaran bodies and airplane fins swam in a loop around the submerged ship. Paul wished he could reach down and touch its metal surfaces.

In a fever to explore further, Paul passed the dome and descended into the city by one of many soaring, curving ramps that led down to broad avenues between tall buildings. The roadway was of the same E-shaped stones he'd seen in the countryside, overgrown with grass and here and there a skinny tree. The avenues were very wide; and the buildings, now broken off as their walls crumbled, must have been many hundreds of feet high.

Tired and overwhelmed, Paul came to a narrow portal in a high wall. There appeared to be grass on the other side, good to sit down on. He entered what must once have been a park, still carpeted with tall green grass. Hedges and trees grew wild everywhere, through which blew a cool, winey wind. Sunlight was filtered by leaves. Amid the greenery he saw tumbled fountains. He saw statues of athletes, of thinkers, of beautiful women. No statues of soldiers or politicians. No religious motifs. The statues of women were especially wonderful, sometimes explicitly, though never grossly erotic; mostly radiantly virginal and ethereal. The athletes were always caught in snapshots of motion and were gracefully proportioned. The philosophers, or thinkers, whatever they were, were infrequent. These were tucked into hidden recesses in hedges and small back courtyards, whereas the athletes and women were prominently displayed on the open slopes of the park. There was no stylization; no transcendence or transfiguration. The statues were so lifelike that Paul had the unsettling feeling of being in a landscape peopled with gray, immobile Avamishans.

He saw no more bearded figures; but the large eyes of those he'd seen earlier followed him in memory. Their faces stared after him enigmatically with small black pupils in white sclera signifying heightened emotion, perhaps amazement, perhaps fury, perhaps some alien emotion unknowable to Earth people except in feverish and hallucinatory dreams.

He lingered in the park as long as he felt he could contain his appetite. The blissful, unreal landscape created a sense of bitter-sweet longing. Still, amid decay, the statues and their environment strove for perfection in all things. Paul sat down in a grove of trees and opened a can of precious rations. After eating, he felt exhausted. He dozed off briefly.

Awakening with a start, he felt almost as if some outside power was acting upon him. It was a feeling like when Ongka had first drugged him. This was something inherent in the park itself. There was a hypnotic quality, a sense of longing for perfection, for otherness than self, for immortality. Even after all these centuries, he felt the longing for the stars that these people must have felt. Maybe it was the eyes and faces of the statues, the shape of the rolling landscape, the attitudes of the bending, running, whirling athletes, the juxtaposed implications of languidly erotic women and lively sun-smiling girls. The great head of a philosopher sat tilted, hidden in the shadows of wild hedge. Any minute now, those eyes would turn to look at him.

Paul tore himself away from the park. He ran out through the portal, relieved to be once more out on the green, open, mind-ripped avenues. The drugged feeling disappeared.

He realized he had forgotten his canteen in the park. He did have his rifle. Let the canteen stay. Like everything else in the park, if he left it there a thousand years, it would still look as though he had left it only yesterday. He did not want to enter the park alone again today.

He came to the portals of a mile-long building. No telling how tall the building might once have been, because its superstructure had collapsed onto the street. Its jagged ramparts still stood at least three hundred feet high.

Full of curiosity and still tingling from his experience in the park, Paul entered, but cautiously. The floor had crumbled and was overgrown with soft, spongy sod. In the lobby a fountain emptied into a cracked basin. Paul bent down and drank from the water. Then he looked up and gasped, water dribbling down his chin. The ceiling was a dome several stories over his head. At first he thought the dome was supported by pillars. The pillars weren't pillars but statues forty feet tall and taller, of slender, long-robed men and women. No beards; all Ongka's kind. These were more likely images of important citizens. Perhaps the bearded ones on the other building represented mythological gods. The leading citizens of Avamish portrayed here had flat introverted smiles and clenched hands. They conveyed a sense of desperate, gigantic wanting and waiting.

Paul's feet echoed on intact tiles as he walked through another portal into a whispering, cathedral-sized hall whose ceiling was lost in gloom. This was no place of reverence. Everything suggested to Paul an exhilaration of the senses. He found the elephantine statuary in the larger hall vapid and subesthetic by Earth standards. Everything in the building was gigantic in scale, to daze the senses, to quash thought, to create an effect in the Avamishan mind and body that Paul could not even guess at. It only served to depress him.

He labored up huge steps to a mezzanine. He looked down at where he had stood a minute ago, and almost had the impression he could blink and see himself looking up at himself. Crazy, this place. Playing tricks on his mind. He began to suspect the walls themselves had some telepathic aura. He walked through echoing corridors whose sense of disproportion gave him vertigo. He reached only elbow level to the muscular, somber-faced, rippling statue of a wrestler grappling with some shapeless horror like a cloud. The space, between troubled-looking eyes, was almost a meter. The gaze was startled, as if the wrestler could barely contend with the nightmare in his arms, but already stared at an even greater nightmare beyond that.

Paul's walk brought him back to the mezzanine. A maze of rooms and galleries ran off in all directions. In the rooms were colossi. This was truly a building of statues. In one room was an ethereal, child-faced beauty, nude, with an overly massive torso and heavy arms and legs that to Paul seemed to defeat the purpose of the facial presentation, to contradict or overwhelm the airiness and purity.

In another room was a forty-foot tall athlete whirling a discus with airfoils on it.

Room after room had figures in it, huge and somehow weary, as if their weight could not overcome the gravity that bound them to whatever their tragedy was.

Paul left the building feeling drained and slightly nauseous. His own erotic and esthetic standards had been assaulted and offended, overwhelmed and numbed.

Even the size of the building oppressed him and he hurried away from it, back toward the encampment. He felt badly in need of human company. Faraway on the hillsides he could see smoke from the natives' tent city. He jogged in the that direction on the crumbling, deserted avenues. Wind keened desolately, just audibly, around his ears, and he often looked back over his shoulder. His spine crawled and he was glad to get out of the dead city's heart.

Just seeing the living natives cheered him up. On his way back Paul found a fresco of life in ancient Avamish.

The scene was off-hand and lacked any elements of tragedy or comments about the seriousness of life.

Several Avamishans sat in a cart in a variety of bored or anxious poses, as if they were on a rumbling bus.

The right rear wheel of the wagon ran through a puddle of water.

It splashed an Avamishan lady on the sidewalk.

The lady was depicted in the act of staring with a surprised, angry look over her shoulder at her dress, which she grasped with one hand and pulled away slightly.

Nearby, two young dandies were caught in the act of winking at each other and pointing to the splashed lady.

An Avamishan boy farther along the street, unaware of the lady's plight, busily played an instrument like triple pan pipes.

The boy sat on the curb.

A young girl with a sweet face was enraptured by his music. The girl, like the lady, wore a chlamys that demurely covered both shoulders.

There was still a freshness, an innocence here, that belied the frank but joyless motions of the statues he'd seen in the building of gigantic art.

Thinking of Licia, he let out a yell and ran up the post road.

33. New World—Year 3301

Something was wrong. Very wrong.

Tynan sat staring sullenly into the smoking embers where a fire had been. The fire was gone. The fire was out. Licia, standing at the edge of the woods, looked over her shoulder. Her eyes were tear-swollen. Her face was pale and bleak.

"We're leaving this morning," Tynan said.

"Come on," Paul pleaded, a lump in his throat.

"We decided," Licia said looking desperately at Tynan and defiantly at Paul.

Tynan's eyes were briefly averted. He still stared at the embers, not of the fire, but of his life with Nancy. When Tynan finally did look again at Paul, his gaze was direct, unblinking, and brutal. Tynan lifted his gaze out of Nancy's coffin and his eyes found nothing consequential in Paul. "We have decided, Menard, that we are going back to the village."

"We?" Paul's stomach fluttered. He felt helpless, murdered, as if he had been assaulted again by a thrown rock. He looked at the truth revealed in Tynan's eyes. He looked at Licia, and the same truth was there. Licia's face mirrored guilt, fear, defiance, love, resentment, longing, pity. In the end it did not matter anymore, and all three knew that. It was the Aerie way. He was being despoused. No, he had been despoused. Just saying so made it so.

Paul realized that he had met his aliens. Licia was galaxies away.

Tynan rose. "We listened to you, and here we are. Only three of us left, for all we know, and you bring us here. We need to be in the village, Menard, where we are safe. Where we can multiply. You are not fit to lead us."

Blindly, Paul struck at Tynan. Licia stood out of reach beyond Tynan. Paul caught Tynan's fist on his own face, reopening his wound. He cut his knuckles on Tynan's teeth, stunned his hand all the way up his wrist on Tynan's cheek bone. They rolled on the ground, equally matched, and finally separated. Tynan dabbed at a bloody lip. "I always wondered if I could take you. You are strong."

Paul ignored him. "Why, Lish?

"Oh Paul." She sat down and cried, face in her arms on her knees. She would not come near him, and he did not go to her. Tynan was between them, but that did not matter just then. His pride mattered. And his stunned acceptance.

Licia finally answered: "Paul, we are so far away, from Aerie law. You have made yourself a stranger to me."

"I what—?"

"You can't see yourself. Obsessed. Driven. With the mound, the city, all these things that don't matter as much as our safety. But it's more than that. I am the only woman left. I have to bear children, or we are finished. This is not about love, or sentiment. Or your feelings. Or my feelings."

Tynan produced his rifle in one lightning move and pointed it at Paul's heart. "It's business, Menard. Work. And I'm not allowing any triangles. It's me and her."

"Licia, I'm giving you a chance—."

"No Paul, I'm so sorry—."

"Menard, you know what has to be, you of all people."

34. Old World—Year 2299

"Menard—for the love of God!"

Paul hurt inside as he looked out of the thick Aerie window. He looked at, but didn't really see, the snow plains, the way they threw themselves against the cold bluish mountain crags.

Krings was on his knees, sobbing. "Menard, for the love of God. She is all I have left."

35. New World—Year 3301

Paul lay in a cold sweat staring up at the alien moons. The alien wind moved about him and through him as if he were suddenly lacking all substance. And he did lack all substance. Despoused, he had no soul anymore.

At first his thoughts whirled about. They revolved slower and slower. At last his thinking was nearly as still and cold as the bright revolving constellations above.

Conquest. SheuXe's enigmatic, smiling face appeared before him. Paul stared into the memory bitterly. For the first time he saw SheuXe not as his benevolent, wise friend, but as a brilliant and heartless schemer. An Aerie man.

Aerie law. Paul gripped his head in final immense realization. He had been trying to create a non-Aerie by Aerie rules. Conquest, SheuXe had insisted. So unlike SheuXe. And yet maybe truly SheuXe, ultimately. Aerie law was harsh and arbitrary, but necessary for survival. Harsh unequivocal laws served best to deal quickly with crises, in a world where crisis was frequent and almost always fatal.

36. Old World—Year 2299

Paul received the call from Licia just as he was about to suit up for an hour of hawk-baiting, the lesser of the avian games. "Paul, can you help me? I've got to find my father. He's disappeared." So he'd begged off from his old school pals and jogged back to the training school. He was hardly surprised, given Krings's behavior lately. He jogged through the sunlit corridors, the ramps crossing from building to building, all enclosed in thick glass. As he ran, he thought only of how to keep her from being hurt, or from somehow turning against him. He was, after all, the man who had finally undone her father by despousing him of her. In these more desperate times, that no longer meant automatic expulsion as it had when the aeries had been overcrowded, but Krings's pride still saw the social catastrophe. He had already been disgraced in his field by losing the battle over whether to try and reclaim the Earth or leave it. He already had no students, and would now be stripped of his teaching position, his Council membership, and his living quarters.

"He's gone," Licia said as Paul arrived at the deep space flight training center. Tynan and Nancy were there, as were quiet Meiling and Peng Wing. "Just you, Paul. Let's go together." So he and Licia walked down into the bowels of the Aerie. "I went to visit him at our home, and he must not have been there in a day or two. I didn't want to call the Constabs. You never know, with his pride the way it is." They walked together, up into the old sprawl, out of the populated neighborhoods. Bit by bit, the echoes of children playing faded. The air under the glass and concrete ceilings became quieter and quieter, and finally almost silent. They entered the dimly lit corridors of the Old Aerie, from the worst days two centuries ago, when millions had clawed their way up into the mountains, and millions of those had died, and the remaining few hundred thousand had had to adopt incredibly harsh rules to survive. The streets here were drab, the houses utilitarian. Long ago, there had been waiting lists. Families had camped for decades on sidewalks, fighting for tent space and cooking rights. Now you could ramble through block after block of deserted homes. Some had not been lived in for 100 years. Here and there, one could still find a rusted vehicle parked by a front door, or a blackened spot where generations of the same family had cooked on the sidewalk. Some of the old street signs of Albuquerque still stood on the odd corner here and there. "This is the house where my father grew up," she said. "People still lived in this neighborhood until about 25 years ago. I was born near here. The hospital is long since closed." She pushed open a plain wooden door, and they entered a warren of small rooms. "Our family lived here for many generations." The place smelled of bad food and leaky pipes. Paint chipped off the walls. A few old posters still stuck to the walls, but overgrown with a purplish mold.

They heard him.

"Father?"

Krings wailed something incoherent.

Paul dashed through the semidark toward the ever-bright kitchen area, Licia pressing from behind. He could feel her breath on his neck, her fists in his back. He could almost feel her heart beating.

Krings squatted in a corner of the kitchen, on the floor. If he had cried here, in the house where he'd grown up, his tears were long dry. He was naked from the waist up, fluffs of white hair around his dangling skin. He'd soiled his pants, but they were so drab and dirty Paul could only dimly tell that there were areas that were darker and wetter than the rest. He sat with his back to the wall, arms wrapped around himself. His face had an utterly vapid expression, and his eyes were bright and blue and utterly trusting like those of a toddler. He looked up, drooling, and said to Licia in a bright little voice: "Hello, Mamma. I good." He repeated in utter sincerity, as if he expected to be picked up: "I good, Mamma. I good boy."

37. New World—Year 3301

Paul stood alone in the dead alien city. It was night time, and he looked up at the stars that wheeled in the black sky. The horizon was an architecture of broken towers and ruined walls, but the stars above shone brightly like windows in a greater skyline. The twin moons clung together, as always, their surfaces swimming with light, and the light softened their craters. The night air was both fresh and sweet, but also mysterious with small musky odors and whiffs of this and that. Suddenly, he was utterly free.

Avamish somehow held the key to the stars. If it was the only thing he accomplished on N60A, it would be to give them the key to the stars. Not for Tynan, or even Licia, but for their children and their children's children.

Strange, that you had to travel light years to find yourself. He lost himself in the rotted, dripping maze of broken houses of Avamish. Suddenly, he was absolved of all debts. He no longer felt compelled to conquer, or even to survive. He was a citizen of the galaxy. Moisture rolled on his face, chilling him.

He barely noticed that night gave way to day.

A morning fog roiled thickly all around.

For once, he felt deadly calm. He had nothing to compromise anymore. It was a feeling of absolute power. He could take the city and shake it until it yielded its secret.

A small detail began to preoccupy him. A matter of life and death; a lost canteen. He was on his own now, and he must have water. He would not let the city defeat him.

Fog brought back the illusion of throbbing city life. He thought of the handsome dignified man with the goblet. He felt Avamishan. Rather than cower in Aeries, man was meant to build great cities that reached to the stars. O SheuXe if you only knew. He felt Chaldean, Sumerian, Zapotecan, Roman, New Yorkan.

Gravity dealt him a blow which brought him back to reality. He stumbled over a log and slid tumbling down an embankment coated with wet mud. He hit hard at the bottom of the ravine. His clothes clung wet and icy as he crawled up onto a dry, solid city street of large stones. Gravity. Of course. The laws were the same here as everywhere else in the universe.

In the still heavy fog, he came to an intersection. He stopped and aimed the rifle. Not far away, where the fog seemed lighter with growing sunlight, a dark figure stood watching him. He lowered the weapon. Ongka. He recognized the dully gleaming copper disk. Fog rolled by, and the figure was gone.

"Ongka!" he cried, searching. "Ongka! Dammit, you brought us here. Play games, will you? Bastard!"

His voice threw a faraway echo among ruined buildings. Only silence answered.

Paul stood there, regaining his breath. He remembered the clockwork. Like SheuXe, Ongka, with his terrible intelligence, had some sort of master plan. The medicus had been toying with them—especially with Paul—ever since their arrival. SheuXe would have been mortified to learn that the new world contained at least one intellect as great as his own, a stone age shaman who understood the workings of the galaxy.

Paul arrived at the space port. Gilt sunlight stabbed through fog molecules, whirling dizzy bright particles around mist-shrouded buildings. Paul passed through the broken memories of star longing. Ongka would make some move soon. Until then, he had to survive. He would have to retrieve his canteen. Remembering how his mind had gone dull in there, he avoided the park as yet, waiting until full daylight.

First, he explored a large building that turned out to be a public bath. The ghostly echoes of his footfalls on tile followed him, traveling away down long high tiled corridors and meeting him again when he passed other doorways. He saw the main pool in a domed hall full of nesting birds. Abundant multi-colored lizards too dwelt in the clear shallow pool water. The lizards hissed and showed rows of serrated teeth as he walked past.

He came to a large office building. A fountain bubbled among pillars in the lobby. In the honeyed sunlight, statues graced odd corners. Everything was businesslike. The lobby opened into a big hall lined on both sides with stone-barred cages. Paul thought of banks or pay offices on old Earth. In one of the cages, entering at random, he found stone office furniture—a tall, graceful stool; a stone safe; a bookcase whose shelves were still stained with the bacteria that had consumed its paper ledgers. On the teller's or accountant's desk was a hydraulic telephone. The speaking orifice extended toward the teller on a stone tube. The listening end was a hand-sized cylinder lying on the desk. A bit of shattered tubing stuck out of it. Why had all this been abandoned?

In the bank cellars Paul found money. The stone coins rattled through his fingers, and he thought that once they must have been well-guarded. His flashlight beam picked out stacked coins on tables. Nearby, he heard the splash of some lizard guarding this hoard. It was not a place to tarry long. On one table was a mound of spongy matter that might once have been paper or wooden money. He slipped one of the cold coins into his pocket. As he did so he heard something breathing nearby and crawling over the stone floor with rasping scales. As he backed up he could feel its cold breath on his hand. He tumbled over backwards, landing in a shallow puddle. He got his hands around something to throw. A stone, he thought. The thing bucked in his hands, twisting this way and that. Another lizard. It had been sleeping in the cold water. Now he saw its teeth flash in the gloom as it arched backwards to bite him. Its split tongue flashed wetly in the dim light. Paul threw it as hard as he could against its mate. How many more were down here? He heard a hiss of reptilian breath and ran as fast as he could, back up into daylight, where he stood with his back to a wall and gasped to get his breath back.

In the upper stories he found sealed offices, many with heavy glass windows overlooking the city still intact. He entered one room that was larger than the rest and had no windows. He waded through an ankle-deep layer of dust and hair that must once have been a carpet. The room contained a large desk—empty, as if the owner had taken its contents with him—and several tumbled, rotted wooden chairs. Against one wall stood shelves piled with bric-a-brac: The dust of manuscripts; empty flower vases; an assortment of stone coins and the spongy remains of wooden money; a stone carving of a whale-like fish. Another wall had once been covered with a cloth tapestry. The cloth was long gone, but a ghostly after-image of rockets and tall buildings remained on the dry stonewall, burned in by the desiccation of old dyes.

As he turned to leave, Paul noticed a strange pattern of designs on a third wall. The wall was citron-colored. On it were fine-ruled white quadrilles, and in many of the quadrilles were variously colored squares of thin foil. Metal foil? Paul bent closer, scratching one off so it stuck to his fingertip. Some conductivity or magnetism in the wall kept them attached. As Paul ran his fingers over the wall, he felt a tingle race through his fingertips, his elbows, his brain. Quickly he withdrew his hand, and the feeling ceased. He touched the wall again, hesitantly, and felt a pleasant jumbled consciousness of something larger than himself and abstract. What was it? He placed one fingertip directly on one foil square. For an instant he perceived a number, 5000, then there was that vapid, white feeling again leaving an aftertaste of feminine pleasantness. It reminded him of the girl with the goblet. He touched a few more squares.

Nothing. Just pleasant white feeling, fading quickly as if to recharge.

Then, from a brown square, he picked up a fragment of thought—not words, but pure thought, delivered in report-like efficiency: "Ang Shovi Geyser 500 ixtl sha output average in year 607 and..." (white, fading). Paul put his hands to his head. Only his experiences with Ongka prevented him from reeling about in shock.

He touched another square. Nothing, He noticed that the floor before him was littered with light-colored squares that had fallen off. Apparently the darker squares were stronger and more empathic. As he touched another dark brown square, a thought stung his fingertips and expanded behind his eyes: "...With Xnl Iplon owes 400 bactrs to City Treasury..." (fade). When Paul put his fingertips on the square again, he received only a faint pulse saying "400" and then white dim-out. Apparently, it took a little time for the information squares to build up their charge again. From the air? Perhaps that was why this room had no windows. Perhaps ... anything. Paul lightly made a sweep with his hands over the wall. It was like listening to a hundred radio stations at once.

Some of the squares had lost their imprint but still emitted a powerful white field. Paul seemed to understand the foreign words. Bacter was a unit of currency, ixl was a measure of volume, sha was time.

In a stroke of admiration, Paul realized that this wall was a sort of corporate progress chart. The room was an executive conference room.

He touched another square and its fragmentary message was: (noise) "...transfer credit allowance of 70 spenter type 45 fuel to Moon II launch station under armed guard. Anticipate conversion to non-spenter money base if metals found on Moon II as hoped. Star Base One alleviate shortage..." (noise...noise...).

Paul's flashlight was growing dim and he pulled his hand away with deep regret. In this place, if those delicate charges could survive but a few more weeks, he could learn a lot about ancient Avamish. The most exciting thing was that they had indeed reached space, and Paul wanted to see N60A from orbit once more. If it had been done before, it could be done again.

He felt elated when he returned to the street, but suddenly he felt a twinge of loneliness. He had nobody to tell of his discovery.

A cursory probe of several other buildings turned up more of the telepathic boardroom charts, but none quite as explicit or well preserved. He did find the unreadable remains of tons of paper. Apparently, metals were necessary for telepathic reporting, witness Ongka's disc.

He found a library. The building was oblong, of light-green stone like a marble. Its windows were broken. In the main entrance a few shards of stone door still hung on their hinges. The interior of the library was a barren, scoured disaster. The ceiling had been constructed of many skylights, all of them broken by now, so that the elements had erased all of the precious books.

As Paul stood hungering amid the empty shelves he heard a clattering noise. He thought he caught the faint echo of departing footsteps as he whirled about with his rifle ready, but he heard nothing now. Shaking, he called out: "Ongka!"

Silence.

Slowly he relaxed. Probably a bird or other animal. Maybe the crumbling of a piece of mortar.

Nothing.

He was alone.

When he left the library the sunlight was long and golden. The city, like its cup-raising ghosts, steeped in eternal melancholy.

And now Paul was part of that tranquil death, that silent slow fading.

He hurried from building to building, faster and faster, as if to outrun himself. To outrun the black hollow in his heart now that he was despoused. He was in a suburb of wealthy palaces and homes beyond the starport. Thoughts of Licia pursued him. The thought of her tormented him.

He ran across the grounds of a deserted palace. He bumped into something; tumbled a small statuette off of its pedestal so it crashed in pieces on the tiled walkway. The dead city surrounded him with walls of resentful silence.

The palace had been gutted by fire. What remained of its walls were blackened. In a corner he found a round thing encased in moss and when he looked at it he found it was a skull that had been smashed by some heavy bladed thing, an ax maybe. He remembered the skulls in the mound near Akha. So there had been fire and violence in the decline of Avamish after all. Paul ran through the ruin like a maddened dog, shattering anything the building's destroyers had left unbroken. Licia! The pain—There was a kitchen and he heaved chinaware over his head so that for long seconds he was enveloped in a tinkling nose as loud and constant as rain. He ran down a long corridor. At the end of the corridor he dimly perceived a glassless window open to a patch of azure sky. He screamed and wanted to ...

(noise...xxxx...noise...xxmnorxmnt...noi...noise····xxmann rxxxx xxxmannr...noise)

...but he stopped. He leaned with his back to the wall and gaped for air. What were they doing to him? The city was alive with stray telepathic thoughts, many of them black and unpleasant. He slumped into a squatting position to gather his mind back together.

Must not—must not feel this way.

The sky was hot and hazy when Paul stood in the space complex again.

Behind him lay the wealthy suburbs, destroyed violently centuries ago. Beyond those suburbs lay the open land, the today and the tomorrow of a city steeped in yesterday. He would only have to begin walking. It would be like a death. He would walk and walk until he fell down and became part of the soil. It would be a journey with no return. But no. The city yet held him back, demanding that he delve into its mystery.

Soon, night would fall again.

He looked north and saw the smoking kilns of the tent city. Right then he decided what he would do that night. Taking a drink from a fountain, he began the long march through the city amid the heat and haze of late afternoon. Despoused, alone, he was no longer of Earth. He could now make the city part of him. He and the city would soak up each others' souls and understand one another. He was now the last Avamishan.

38. New World—Year 3301

Despite himself, he went the long way around, coming up on the post road where he'd last seen Tynan and Licia. Their camping spot was abandoned. Licia was gone. Gone with Tynan, back to Akha. That part of his life was over. He hid his meager baggage (sleeping bag, shelter, rifle, pistol) and crept down toward the natives. He must see what it was they came here to do. There was another reason too, a hunger, that he could not voice. Maybe it was just the desire to be with people again, even if they weren't exactly people.

The tent city was cool with amber evening when Paul crept through the thick woods and underbrush. Lonely evening wind blew coolly around him in the high grass. He was hungry and realized he had forgotten to eat that day. The rich aromas of native cooking permeated the air around the tent city.

The natives were in a celebratory mood. They ate and drank and sang boisterously. Drums rumbled across the valley as night fell. He watched hundreds of milling dark bodies from his vantage point. Still, new arrivals kept appearing amid rounds of warm, noisy applause. Dozens of makeshift kilns blazed in the tent city. The twin moons shone brightly. No evidence of Licia or Tynan; he could be sure now that they had left for Akha.

He worked his way around the perimeter, ever afraid to be spotted. From the kiln area he heard piping and drumming. He could almost feel the thud of dancing feet. He heard the sharp breaths of straining dancers. Their laughter sounded as if it were all around him, and he clung closer to the shadows.

At the downhill end of the tent city he came upon a scene of torches and hammering. He saw workmen drinking heavily, sweating and swearing around some indeterminate labor. In a corner of the work area was a pile of unopened flasks. Several men worked on a wooden box big enough to hold several men standing up. Paul stared in puzzlement. An older man worked off to one side assisted by a younger man. The old man was white-haired and brawny—used to physical exertion all of his life. He hammered at an object while his slim, long-haired assistant held extra tools and a brace of nails for him. The old man worked feverishly as if in a great hurry and resisted by the object of his labors. The assistant suggested something that Paul could not hear against the noise from the other workers. The old man shook his head disparagingly at whatever the suggestion might have been. He uttered a command, and both men labored to lift the object on its side. Dull as he was by now from tiredness, Paul instantly recognized that he was looking at a wheel.

A wheel!

It was the first native-made wheel he had yet seen. He had thought that the wheel was a lost Avamishan art. Yet here it was—a thick wooden disk about three feet in diameter, reinforced with thick planks. The wheel stood on its side and the old man pounded more stone nails into it in a hopeful but uncraftsmanlike fashion. Paul gaped. He was watching a group of stone age men building wooden wagon wheels. Why then had they not brought their heavy burden of stone wine jars to the tent city in wagons? Surely it made no sense to build wagons after the work was done; unless something was going to happen here; something that had perhaps been commonplace in ancient Avamish?·Paul tried to think it through. After all, the natives had models for wagons buried all around their villages, only awaiting some renaissance. Was there a Petrarch, a Leonardo, a SheuXe, a renaissance man waiting to appear among these people?

Paul stared at the drunken men who worked so hard at these tasks that had no place in their normal village lives.

Involuntarily, Paul peered up at the surrounding hillsides, but he detected no sign of one tiny, warm campfire. His sudden change of position still shocked him; he had to keep reminding himself that Licia was gone forever from his life.

One of the workmen stepped into darkness and Paul heard him urinate while humming to himself. Paul stole closer. He was thirsty, and those piled jars looked inviting. He stole two little ones. They felt cold and heavy, and they clinked unnervingly as he lifted them from their mates. The singing and hammering covered whatever noise he made. He stole away.

He found a distant, high vantage point. There, he sat in misery and drank. Below him he watched the smoky, noisy gathering. The wine was sour-sweet and reminded him of Akha. For the first time, he wished he'd listened to both Tynan and Licia, and stayed in

Akha. Maybe she'd been right—they'd been safe there. What a fool he'd been. How he'd screwed up a mission that had taken a thousand years of time, 25 light-years of travel, and the last surviving six human lives. The apple wine smelled pungent. He drained the first jug quickly. The wine gripped his unfed body as he pried the swollen cork out of the second stone vessel. He stared long and hard down into the tent village but could not find any trace of Ongka, Auska, Amda, even bumbling Dunda. Halfway through the second quart or so he rose with drunken resolve. He would go down and announce himself to the natives. If they killed him right there, so what. He crawled and stumbled back downhill. It went quickly, and pretty soon he stood swaying, jug in hand, gathering up his courage.

Then he noticed a small wooden shack. The wood was freshly cut and planed, and held in place with a combination of wooden dowels, stone nails, and leather thongs. It was a neat piece of work. Instead of a door, it had flap of foul-smelling hide; probably fresh off some hairy kill. It was unguarded. Paul staggered closer, set his jug down, and looked inside. Pitch black. Smelled awful. He felt about with one hand: lumpy, sour-smelling, hard objects. Round— no, cylindrical—he tugged one out and held it in his arms as if it were a baby. It was a rocket about three feet long and two or three inches in diameter, with a long thin dowel for a guide. The rocket was packed in a stiff, resinous cloth sewn together at a seam running along its length, and covered with animal fat. So that was the rancid odor. Paul stood swaying in the night, holding his rocket up to the unamused moons.

He laid the rocket back into the darkness amid its companions. Rocking back and forth on his heels, he lifted the wine jug and took a big draught. He rubbed his hands so that the grease came off onto his torn jumpsuit. The liquor coursed through his body like fire. He felt hungry and wanted to go down into the tent city to get food. He wanted to drink and dance and make love with natives and Auska or someone like her. He staggered along the uneven, winding rim of the bowl of Avamish. He staggered for a long time and could not find his way. Finally, he fell face-first into a bed of soft pine needles and passed out.

He was awakened by the sound of women laughing. His head hurt and he felt nauseous. The sun stood full over the horizon. The women's high, silly laughter sliced through his headache. A group of young girls played tag in the high grass and fragrant flowers, not far down the hill. They were pretty children, naked and blue-brown, with sparkling eyes. Butterflies wandered about. He thought once more of turning himself in. Then he remembered the rockets, and decided he still had some exploring to do.

Oh, but his head hurt. He was famished and weak. He found a broken pipe from which fresh spring water trickled. He put his face to the stone and drank thirstily. Behind him, the girls and the women ran further down the slope, back into camp. He smelled food and tracked down the remnants of their picnic—leaves, cold now, smeared with paste, beans stuck together, bits of bone and gristle, a scrap or two of meat—he was so hungry he devoured pieces of the leaves.

Near the space port, he shot a bounding rabbit-thing. He made a fire and cooked it. He peeled skin and fur off as it cooked, using his knife to bring the giblets to his mouth. The taste and sticky feel of blood brought him to his senses.

He remembered his lost canteen, and headed toward the park. He walked along the edge of a broad avenue. This was a new angle of approach, but all roads led to the star city. The avenue was carpeted with grass. Wind spirits blew loose brush around him. Wind whistled in blank doorways and dark windows.

He crossed a line of trees and stood at the edge of a rectangular expanse big as an airfield. A number of small, low buildings were scattered far apart across the field. Beside each building stood a pillar of solid stone, broken off, the tallest about twenty feet high. Wind soughed through with an empty, eerie effect. As he passed the buildings he looked into several. In one he found a wagon, broken in half, its wheels still attached.

In another building he found bits of petrified hay, along with a few scattered black stone bolts and wheel hoops. In a third building he found stone storage bins; they were empty, except for some broken cups.

All of the buildings were scarred and gouged, as if by bullets or crossbolts. Great violence had occurred here. There were signs of fire. Wooden doors had been bashed in.

In a fourth building Paul found a tangle of skeletons. They lay piled together and had mostly disintegrated. Each skull had been smashed by a heavy object—several times.

The climax of death was ages past. Wind blew remorselessly as Paul crossed the field. Perhaps this had been a market square—who could tell now?

He crossed a tangle of major avenues that led to various parts of the city.

He came, at last, to the place where he had left his canteen. He felt again the oppressive, sun-drunk park silence.

But the canteen was gone.

Someone or something had found it and carried it off. He cursed the statues that were poised as if converging on him. The giant philosopher head in the ground stared at him like an angry schoolmaster.

He yelled "Ongka!" and his voice carried no farther than the nearest tree, the nearest frozen discus thrower.

Near the exit he saw a small stone building he had not noticed the other time. Its walls were concrete, dark gray. The building was octagonal, worn with age, and had no windows. Its roof was intact, consisting of glossy greenish tiles that rose up, pagoda-style, at the corners. All eight sides of the roof rose in the center, converging in a decorative black ball. For some reason, the building made him curious—perhaps literally, judging by the telepathic currents in this weird alien place. He walked around it and found the structure had a stone door with a stone ring in a hinge. The door was closed. He tried the ring, and the door swung inward on silent, oiled hinges. Oiled? He knelt down and touched the threshold, then brought his fingers to his nose. No smell. No oil. Just well-built.

The door might have been closed a thousand years or more. Inside was darkness, dust, dry air. Not a single object—oh! his canteen lay on the concrete floor. Shocked at its migration, he picked it up. It had been nearly empty when he left it. Now it was full. Heavy. He opened it and took a sniff. Fresh water, with a tinge of anise. He remembered the drug he'd been given his first day in Akha. Someone—Ongka?—had filled the canteen, moved it here— why? Why these stalkings, these indirect gestures? Just as indirect as when he had been handed pick and shovel with instructions to dig into the mound.

He stared about him in the gloomy little room in which the only light was sunlight that crept through the open doorway. No furniture, no windows, just a barren room inside an eight-sided stone cylinder about twelve feet in diameter and some ten feet high. Claustrophobic.

But wait! Paul suddenly realized that the walls, the roof, all but the floor, were completely sheathed in metal, in dully pitted copper. He touched the wall briefly. A strong thought ballooned in his mind: "Avamish..." said a young male voice lovingly.

Paul barely noticed that slowly, the door swung shut.

Remembering the thought-squares covering the wall in that dark bank vault, home of lizards, he closed his eyes (it was pitch dark now anyway), steeled himself, and placed both hands flat against the wall. The blast of sights and sounds and smells was immediate and overwhelming.

39. New World—Year 3301

"Oh Avamish," echoed a small girl voice full of admiration and longing.

There were voices filled with love for their city, but also with aching, hopeless melancholy, and Paul felt what they felt, saw what they saw, lived again these moments in their long-ago lives. His mind reeled at the feelings that drowned his senses now. He realized why there was no god on N60A. The city was the supreme hope, the final salvation, the omega and the ultima.

Paul's small human ego rebelled against the complete gratification of the self, the transcendence and glorification of the body and mind and city because there was nothing better to glorify. Nothing more was possible.

He saw all of Avamish as she had once been, from a vantage point as high as the clouds. Her towers and spires rose a mile into the sky, dwindling from massive bases to fine diamond points. Beacons glittered like exploding rainbows in the diamond tips. Paul walked around the entire circumference of the room with his hands held against the wall. He took in the full 360 degree sweep and felt vertigo.

His airship descended toward Avamish. It paddled among the domes and skyscrapers like a whale. Paul looked down and saw an immense dirigible rising from the airfield and when he looked up he saw that he stood in a turret suspended from the side of the passenger bus of a similar aeronautical giant.

Voices were all around him. They pressed him, possessed him, babbled like falling water and rising fountains. There were thousands of voices. Some were deep and tinged with evil, for such was part of nature. Others were child voices bright and full of innocence, for this was also part. There seemed always to be an overtone of one or more voices raised away from the others in an expression if awe, of longing, of bittersweet, supreme ecstasy. The language was Avamishan—similar to Akhan or Shkan; but more fluid, more musical; classical; and Paul understood every word through the telepathic process. It was a cosmopolitan language, tumbling like brook water, a babble easily converted into radio waves and sent across the cosmos.

The avenues below were filled with Avamishans including gentlemen and slaves. The ones with the lighter bluish skin and the silvery hair were the masters. The ones with the darker brownish bluish skin and no spinal hair were the slaves. Again, no bearded figures. There were street urchins and wealthy ladies browsing in markets and swaggering powdered gentlemen and hard-faced, mousy office clerks. White-kilted policemen strutted with tall ivory canes, wearing helmets surmounted by fluffy dulzuri plumes (a languid royal bird of the tidal marshes, symbol of Avamish).

Hydro-power trolleys crawled up the hillsides and urban avenues, or descended just as slowly and carefully under gravitational power. The city had a perennial festive air. Every day was special. Moniam bestibo!

Paul's dirigible landed gently in the field where there would someday be skeletons in a lading house. Nearby another dirigible was already snuggled against its landing pylon, tied to the ground and straining in the wind to rise, to be away. A hundred men unloaded grain from the faraway agricultural empire and another hundred men brought tools and farm machines and city goods to be loaded on wagons.

The skins of the dirigibles shone silver in the clear blue sky. Nearby was an explosion and a flash of light and Paul turned to watch a titanic rocket lift up from the space launch center, headed perhaps for some mining camp on Moon II, or a star-watching base on Moon I, or maybe a metal-rich planet of a star with a poetic name.

Paul watched ropes fall from his own ship. He watched as faces and hands reached out to take charge of the hot air balloon. He smelled baking bread and steaming wash water and animal musk from the market place. He smelled smoke from chimneys and salt water from the sea and millions of acres of wheat across burgeoning farm lands.

"Avamish," chorused the thousand voices in admiration and longing, in hope and hopelessness: "Oh, Avamish!"

Exhausted, its static charge gone, the show came to an end. Paul stood for a long time, leaning against the wall with both hands. He wanted more. He could not get enough. And yet, he was more puzzled than ever. He knew a lot about ancient Avamish now, but not the crucial answers.

Elated, yet disappointed, he stepped outside. Night had fallen. He remembered to pull shut the stone door. Suddenly—and he whirled to look—an explosion smashed his ear drums and rattled his teeth and made the ground shake.

More frightening, though, was the loud bellow that pierced the night sky. It was like the predatory battle cry of some giant dinosaur. It tore at Paul's eardrums, making him roll up and hold his ears. Three times the bellowing sounded, and then silence returned, with just echoes bouncing terrifyingly among the ruins.

40. New World—Year 3301

When he recovered from explosion and the noise, Paul stared at the haunted evening park. He saw spots before his eyes. The statues shimmered mesmerically in a red flickering light. Two of them had beards. Had they been here before? They smiled enigmatically, looking toward the star port with blind marble eyes. Paul suddenly became frantic to rush out of here, back to the wide, wind-blown avenues with their bowed grass.

He ran aimlessly. It was good to run. The night was like cobwebs, warm to brush through. Back to the sack, his mind said, back to the pack, to the back pack ... and his feet pounded on crumbling concrete. There was only one place left to run to, and that was the tent city.

Several times the bellowing sounded, and each time he staggered, holding his ears. The noise was so loud that he was blinded for a few seconds, seeing shapes like black marble sliding before his tortured senses.

A second explosion: the ground shook behind him and lights flashed, briefly teasing daylight back into the night.

Another explosion rocked the ground as he ran up the hill. At last he presented himself in the native camp. Breathlessly bent over with his hands resting on his knees, he half expected to be killed. To his surprise, he was ignored.

Celebrants thronged the post road. The great festival had begun. Paul joined them not knowing what would happen next. Hands were laid on his shoulders and he found himself swept along. It was good to be among people again, good to eat kiln food. An answer was shaping in his mind, but still full of holes, holes that must be filled with information.

There was a flash of light down in the city. It came from the launch center. The ground trembled as a huge fiery object lifted off into the atmosphere.

The natives screamed with delight and terror. Countless arms waved in the night tracing the rocket's course as it rose up over the city and the sea. It disappeared into the heavens, high up, among some clouds.

Each time the bellowing sounded, the natives would cheer and raise their bottles.

Paul started to run down into the city. He ran through the crowds of natives, pushing them gently out of the way. He must know about Avamish, now or never. Behind him he heard warning shouts. He saw dozens of torches flare up in all directions. Then, hearing screams and feeling a rumbling under his feet, he jumped out of the way just in time as a dozen drunken, jug-holding men weaved down the steep incline sitting in a wooden wagon. In their uncomprehending way, they were trying to reenact the daily life of the ancient city! He heard the scraping of stone brakes. The cart rumbling past picked up speed. Paul's hair stood on end as he realized they were getting more wagons ready to race down the hill. In each wagon were men holding a torch in one hand and wine in the other. One of the wagons caught fire and crashed into some boulders and lay smoldering while its occupants dragged themselves to safety. Men and women waving torches chased the wagons on foot. They cheered loudly—a foot race, as it turned out, to see who would be first in towing the carts back up for the next run.

No time for this, Paul thought. He hurried down the hillside away from the road. He stumbled and slithered over piles of round objects that blanketed the hillsides. At first he thought they were skulls. Then he realized that they were empty amphorae. Many were old and mossy. Some lay burst open like stone flowers; grass grew in their guts. "My God," Paul thought with a flash of insight: "How many ages and ages have they been doing this?"

He ran breathlessly through side street after side street until he could see the outlines of the space center clearly in double moonlight.

The ground shook again. A blast of heat hit his face. Thunder followed immediately afterward, penetrating his ears with deafening force.

He heard the bellowing, and this time was too amazed to sense the pain in his ears. As the bellowing smashed through the air, a column of steam issued up, thousands of feet high, from the center of the space port. It wasn't a dinosaur, wasn't some beast, but an artifact of Avamishan manufacture. A siren, calling the natives from all over the planet. Telling them it was time for the festival. Moniam bestibo, he pictured Auska's sweet, wry mouth saying.

Behind him on the hillside he heard frantic cheering.

Another spaceship rose out of the rolling smoke, hovered for several seconds, then streaked away to disappear over the sea.

Not good to be here. Smoke filled the air, and he coughed. His lungs hurt as he forced himself to get closer.

The siren bellowed again, no doubt stirring up birds hundreds of miles away and scaring the whales in the deep sea.

Behind him on the hillside he heard frantic cheering.

Another space ship rose out of the rolling smoke, hovering for several seconds, then streaking away, disappearing over the sea.

Paul's lungs hurt as he forced himself to get closer.

A third rocket went up as he approached the star center. The ground rolled in waves. He fell to his knees but got up and continued running. He smelled acrid smoke. A number of outlying bushes and trees had begun to burn brightly. The air was hot and searing. There was a rumbling in the earth as yet another space craft was made ready for flight. Paul shielded his eyes, striving toward a nest of tiny lights he saw twinkling in the interior of the lizard-infested launch buildings.

The sprawl of grass-covered launch pads flickered with flames falling from the launches. As he got closer, he passed the building that seemed to stand on its fingers. The water in its pools was lit from deep within, murky bottle-green, but bright enough to see the hammerhead sharks circling frantically, their twin catamaran bodies whipping this way and that in terror. Paul saw again the sunken rocket bodies, only in this light it was clear they were covered with barnacles and weren't really made of metal, but of stone.

He came to a narrow stairway. At the bottom was a half-open door, and light spilled out. Down he went, where it was cooler and the air clearer. He found himself in a long dry corridor lit by rows of tiny gas lights along the walls.

His feet echoed on the floor as he ran, closer to the heart of the mystery.

He came to a door of stone bars—open. And another door, also open. He heard a thumping sound, a steady rhythm like that of a room full of washing machines. The light here was a weak pinkish-yellow that he remembered from the deep Aerie—fungals, that could last virtually forever. He ran one finger along the purple wall, leaving a wavering smear. He smelled his fingertip and gagged; dry smell of mushroom earth. The corridor turned into stairs again, sloping downward, curving to the left and then the right. The machine noise grew louder, the air warmer, thicker, so that he almost wanted to hold his ears.

As he continued descending, there was a sudden change. The light merged from sickly pink into insect amber and then into iodine blue. The walls turned mauve, then reddish blue. The light-giving fungus became patchy, and the surfaces around him were not stone but metal. He touched the ancient brassy surfaces, running his fingertips through the pits and corrosions that had occurred over the ages. The surfaces curved gently emerging from rock and losing themselves again in rock. He smelled something—food, he thought. The kilns. How homey. How human. But there were other whiffs and smells and stinks in the air—sulfur, iodine, methane. A factory, Paul thought, listening to the relentless machinery that sounded almost like a human heartbeat.

He heard the piercing cry of an animal larger than the zeppelin whales.

It was a whistle from an organ pipe throat, a bellow at the stars.

Down here in these primordial corridors, he saw the images of the long-dead spacefarers. They had loved to make pictures of themselves. They looked not quite like Earth people, and not quite like Avamishans. Some looked a bit like Hindu gods, with red faces and extra arms; others looked more Chinese, perhaps, round and smothered in their wrappings, with happy laughter at some enigmatic situation of 10,000 or 100,000 years ago. Whoever they had been, they were so long ago that they made the ancientness of this dead city a matter of yesterday, of an hour ago, by comparison.

Paul ran on. Free, a citizen of the galaxy, he jogged without fear down the stone and metal corridors. The fungal lighting gently guided him. Its violet glow made the smooth stone floors seem carpeted with photons. Firefly insects swarmed like passing stars, and he brushed through their humming nebulas. The spattered his face coolly, like fresh water. He caught a whiff of anise. On a hunch, he touched the wall and tasted what was on his fingertip. It was the same thing he'd drunk that first day in the village. Not an herb picked from their gardens, but a substance that grew here in the heart of Avamish. He laughed, wiping the condensation from his face, feeling clockwork knowledge boiling up omnipotently in the unused chambers of his brain.

He followed the smells of cooking and the thumping grew closer and louder. The light changed again, more into amber, and then into sallow yellow like the cooler part of a burning sulfur match. The corridor was crossed by other corridors, and they all ran to a mezzanine of stone and metal overlooking a great gallery. He arrived at the parapet (a wrought iron thing, made, not begotten, full of chaos, no two hoops or squares repeating the same pattern) and leaned on it, catching his breath, trying to make sense of what he saw.

First he was confounded by machines that hung in the air. They were the source of the lumpa-thumpa sound. Brittle old wheezing gadgets, weeping steam, shaking as they pumped air down to the factory floor through leaky leather hoses.

Figures moved everywhere down there, completely covered in light, loose-fitting suits. They were natives, Paul felt sure, each also wearing a kind of glass helmet. The helmets were opaque, colored almost like tarnished copper, but with clear face areas. Each hose ran down to the top of a helmet; no helmet without its hose. What could it mean?

Though the ceiling above was pitch-black, fading upward and lost in stone vaults, the light in the gallery itself was a pleasant citron, like flower petals glimpsed through a wet shower door of wavy glass. As Paul learned to ignore the noisy machines that hung in the air before him, he was able to make more sense of the scene below.

The floor of the gallery was regular, manufactured, not natural. Probably metal, blackened with age, but shiny, coppery, where generations of feet trod in ritual motions. The floor was roughly oval, about 500 feet from long end to long end, maybe half as wide, just big enough not to be claustrophobic. Scattered across the floor were tables, work benches, shelves, machines, conveyor belts, stone rollers. Moving down the rollers were big composite tubes, paper-thin metal/stone alloy, like the sunken rocket body that was home to catamaran sharks. Men and women mixed the fuel together—nitrogen dioxide probably, fertilizer, cousin of nitroglycerin—and sewed it in membranes. The sausage shapes moved down their own conveyors, joining the rocket bodies, packed, loaded, sealed, and ready for the next step. Paul gazed toward the far end of this strange cathedral and saw men without helmets—they were about 20 feet higher than floor level, and about 20 feet below Paul's eye level—hoist a finished rocket into a standing position atop a shallow platform, a kind of triangular recess or corner.

Already, the fierce bellowing of the siren cut through the atmosphere. He understood now—it was a release of volcanic steam, the same steam that had powered factories like the foundry they'd found near the river gorge. The ancient Avamishans of a thousand years ago had unlimited power.

The rocket on its pedestal was a slim cylinder about thirty feet high, with a cone shaped nose, and small fins at the bottom end. The men jumped down from the platform. Paul watched at the platform began to turn. It was a kiosk, sort of like those revolving doors he'd heard of in ancient hotels. The platform turned slowly, and the rocket rotated out of sight around a corner, while a new empty niche appeared. Already a new rocket was almost ready to lift onto this platform. Production was in high gear, evidently; Paul wondered how many days the festival—moniam bestibo, he fondly recalled Auska saying—lasted; probably until they ran out of rocket fuel. Or rockets.

There was a tremendous growl from the other side of the mountain as the rocket caught fire. The chamber was sealed tight, and no exhaust gases leaked in. It had taken thousands of years to get this production line perfected, Paul thought. He could picture the rocket, sitting in its launch tube, at first immobile, then bathed in an increasingly intense plasma of burning fuel, and finally propelled screaming into the atmosphere—to where? Moon I? Moon II? The whales across the horizon? From the night city into the day sea on the other side of the world?

Probably nitrogen atmosphere down there, he figured. Minimize corrosion, explosion danger. They had these old machines that pumped a constant supply of breathable air into their helmets, expelling the old air, which then floated away in the bath of nitrogen gas. Had to keep refreshing the air, not just to breathe, but to prevent nitrogen sickness.

Paul became aware of the figures surrounding him. His head swam with the anise drug as he turned, arms swaying drunkenly, to survey the circle of dark figures wearing round copper disks. He tried to talk, but no words came out. Words were not necessary. He could feel them gathering their thoughts, for they were about to think with him.

As he sank to his knees, arms grasped him at the elbows to steady him. He recognized Amda, Ongka, the shaman from Shka, but there were many others he did not know. They led him down a long narrow corridor of brightly twinkling tile walls lit by gas lights like the ones they had found in the way station on their way to Shka. The tiles were white, the lights strangely match-like, blue at their hottest, then yellow, fading into tall red cones.

They took him to a dark room containing what looked like a doctor's examining couch and a table. On the table lay several items he recognized, including the control panel the hunters had brought home to Akha that early night. They helped him onto the leather surface of the examining table and draped a sheet over him for warmth. Still, he shivered. The drug made you sick. He thought he must be feverish. Then he felt sweat break out on his forehead. He felt female hands, gentle, with a sponge. Warm clear water. He looked up. Auska. She gazed into his eyes with concern. She wore a copper disk.

The medicus men gathered around the table. Each laid a hand on Paul. They all stared into his face, and he involuntarily found himself relaxing, opening up like a pool of water, from opaque to translucent to transparent. He became a rocket body and his struggling thoughts were catamaran sharks as they dove into the pools of who he was.

He felt again the spell of Ongka's mind, only this time it was magnified by the power of several minds acting upon his own. He managed to croak in a dry voice: "Why?" Now, at last, the time had come for a meeting between Earth and Avamish. It was time to find out why. Why all this? Why the Senders, when their city stood empty. What future for the people of both worlds?

The magic of the eight or more glittering metal disks drove away all shame, all privacy, all secrets, even the mysteries he kept from himself. The disks were ranged in a circle over him. Faces peered at him from over the disks.

A mind reached down to touch his, gently; it was Ongka. "Hello, friend."

Fearlessly, Paul stared back. All the walls were gone and Ongka probed Paul's mind while Paul found himself, for the first time, at liberty to explore the shaman's thoughts. He found power, but more, he found fear and confusion and he could not say why. But there were also warmth, concern; more than anything, a desperate hope. He recognized the yearning of murmur and singing from his balloon flight in the octagonal chamber in the park. "Oh Avamish!" cried a young girl. "Avamish, our Avamish," sang a choir of robust male voice rising amid organ music.

Paul was surrounded by a wall of minds. Each mind was a cell. Each was separate territory but interlocked with all of the others. Their combined power mastered him completely and yet it was a delicate, gentle power, surgical in its skill to dissect without destroying. And Paul felt a new power of his own. He could not master his own telepathic process, but stern, friendly minds helped him to project: what? "What is the nature of you?"

The greatest of them was a medicus from Avamish itself, named Dauli, and now Dauli took charge. The other minds stepped back and Dauli's simple, clear, razor-sharp thoughts entered Paul. In Dauli, Paul read the terrible truth, and he wanted to cry. He felt an overwhelming horror at his own mortality. He felt the horror of man's vertigo on the brink of the eternity of time and space. He saw the meaning, the summing-up, of Avamish now that nearly everything possible was said and done and after three thousand years since the founding of the city the end of Avamish was near. No, that had already happened long ago. Another thousand years had passed. Time meant nothing to Avamish.

Dauli let out a great, ironic mental laugh. He imprinted on Paul a sense of what it was to be Avamishan: he demonstrated the power and glory of his birthright. With deadly playfulness he took Paul completely into his power. Paul's soul was lifted kicking and screaming out of its physical context. Dauli laughingly threw him into free fall spinning and glittering with wet reds and grays and whites. Dauli's mental power was like that of a master of the martial arts, smooth and practiced and undefeatable.

Paul's entire nervous system was like one exposed nerve. He was tossed and tumbled terrifyingly through caverns and passages while Dauli examined minutely the very essence of what Terran Man was all about. Not a miserable detail of Paul's racial memory was left untouched everything came into play... :*:*: Gregory, SheuXe, Aeries:*:*:New York, Sumer, Akkad:*:*:Egypt, Rome, NASA, UNASA, CANUSAMEX:*:*: the clouds:*:*:...

Fear raised its slithering saurian tongues. Terror clashed its foamy teeth. Horror's glazed, wide eyes stared. Hatred's insane eyes bored down on Paul with a sound like that of a pin slowly grinding its way through a struggling beetle... :*:*:...Paul soared howling and thrashing through a black lightless void at the pit of which Death's putrescent worms squirmed and tangled like tripe... :*:*:.... :*:*...He stood helplessly atop a ruined wall overgrown with grass and weeds. Beside him stood Dauli and Ongka and Amda. They pointed toward the post road leading away from Avamish. Two figures walked there, Tynan and Licia. Tynan slid his arm down her back and caressed the curve of her rear. She reached up with both arms and pulled his head close to hers for a passionate kiss... :*:*:...The truth, Dauli lasered into Paul's soul, the truth!

Paul emerged in a place even more terrible... :*:*:..Loneliness. His momentum left him sliding over a plain of ice where frozen stalactites jutted up through gravely-abrasive snow crystals. He stared at a starless, moonless blue-black sky in which the last stars had died of cold. He saw the empty shell of a ruined Aerie imprisoned for eternity in an icy cobweb...its empty black windows stared upon him like skull eyes, asking, accusing...*:*:...

But then...

...J+O+Y+O+U+S W+A+R+M+T+H showered him with relief. More than an explorer, Dauli made things he found wrong right and good again with the delicate hands of a master technician. Paul rejoiced reaching for a warm breast and its milk was sweet as hay, fresh as beach towels in mother's closet for going to the sandy lake under glass ceilings in the Aerie. Blood rained through Paul in a yellow and red shower that fed every cranny and every corpuscle and was full of light, X-rayed with Mediterranean sunshine (oh gone Earth! Oh Earth, my Earth!), each droplet of blood becoming a rainbow wheel of stained glass...and together all the rainbow wheels made a mosaic of infinite dazzling choruses of light...

"Avamish," said a man from one or two thousand years ago. "Oh Avamish," a woman answered. Paul heard lute music, the tinkle of cymbals, the rubbing clatter of a sistrum, as a boy's reedy voice recited poetry in sussurant classical Avamishan. Crystal goblets tinkled around a table and Paul felt himself toasting a new bride, who bore one nipple exposed and was beautiful as a Polynesian sunset. She was the young girl from the tomb of the ascending rockets. He heard the thunder of rockets as a space ship thundered and blazed up into the night sky. Paul could not remember if that would be the troop ship to Orion or the botanic barge for Eridani or the evening luxury passenger liner to Fomalhaut or the mail run to Altair...

Dauli tore the fabric of illusions away from Paul's dazzled eyes like a conjurer unconjuring. Paul looked at Dauli hurt and resentful. Twelve minds caressed him slowly back to the white-noise level of consciousness. Slowly the opiate of illusion yielded the truth, the bittersweet truth of what Avamish and Earth might both have been but were never able to become.

Just as Earth had perished in its clouds, so Avamish was a dream of what never had been. Every year, the natives still came to revel in a fool's religion, an impossible dream. They came because their ancestors had also come each year to marvel at the city of dreams.

There had, in truth, never been a city of the stars. There had never been an empire or space flight or a single moon base. All of Avamish had been a wonderful story, a celebration, a continuous drama whose actors were the entire population of the world. The planet lacked metals and there was no escape from its gravity. No need for a city or a star port. The land and climate were good and society was agrarian. But the spirit was not satisfied with peace and plenty. Over the centuries, a technology of stone developed and was refined to untold heights. Science, philosophy, art, these had no physical boundaries. Avamish had its own Newton, its Aristotle, its Gauss, its Einstein, its SheuXe. The philosophers and engineers built a great city and called it Avamish, which meant Our Journey. Still not satisfied (why be?) Avamish had looked to the stars. But it could not reach them. Especially tantalizing was the fact that Moon II was practically made of iron. Just out of reach, sorry.

At the height of its splendor, Avamish was an industrialized society comparable in many ways to Europe in the late 1800's. Stone and wooden ships patrolled the seas, fishing and trading. Zeppelins plied the air. Steam-powered trucks and buses traversed a network of post roads covering both continents of the planet. All roads led to Avamish.

Where physical progress left off due to the lack of metals, spiritual longing kept on. The thirst for star flight was unquenchable. On Earth, the dreams of fantasists led to technological realities. On N60A, the dreams continued and were never more than dreams.

A pseudo space technology complete with would-be engineers, astronauts, bureaucrats, politicians, clerks, and manual laborers came into existence. All the world came to see and be part of the dream, the drama, of what could have been. Of what was promised would one day be reality. It became a religion. But the seeds of undoing existed in a false dawn, the flowering of unreality as reality. Avamish was a hope without substance or fulfillment. Convolution and involution brought disease to her arts and sciences. Light, graceful architecture yielded to buildings and statues of gargantuan proportion and clumsy balance. Elephantism set in. Exhaustion followed soon after.

The city became a tired dream that taxed the entire planet. Eventually the country mice rebelled against the city mice. A coalition of farmers and slaves stormed the city and burned it, killing all its inhabitants except a few who hid in secret underground passages. These kept the dream alive. The wonder of Avamish remained as a sort of afterglow. Technology was sealed into mounds, put back into the embrace of the earth, forbidden. In time, enmities were forgotten. The taller, lighter Avamishans with silvery hair, like Auska, reconciled with the darker, shorter ones of the spinal manes and bald heads. The warriors who had sacked and burned Avamish had borne, painted on their faces and over their heads, a white stripe symbolizing the simple village gods of the wheat, the kiln, the orchards that brought forth apples and heady liquor.

Still today, having long forgotten the nature of the city, the natives made a regular pilgrimage of meat and wine. Each time, Dauli and his native technicians put on a great show for them. Amda and his youthful companions were the next generation of medicuses in training.

Paul, floating in this bath of information, this white nowhere, felt Dauli nudging him, mind to mind. There was more. To really understand the nature of Earth, of Avamish, he had to look deeply again. Deeper than before. Deeper.

There he saw it. The ancient spaceship. Crashed. Dauli showed him a picture: Black outer space spattered with stars. Ships. Ancient ships. They had been to Earth, to Avamish, to a million other points. Time meant nothing to them, these ancient people who had left settlers on a million primitive but lovely gardens of Eden. They were indirectly, by default, in a sense the real Senders. They had conquered time and space. They had only not conquered themselves, for that was a fundamental law of the universe. All things that are born must grow old and die. Stars, planets, living things, all are bound by the natural processes. The ship, Dauli said, stayed behind when the Ancient Ones disappeared. (Where are they now?) We do not know. They may have died out. They may come again tomorrow. They travel through time as readily as they travel through space. They visited earth during your Ice Ages. (How do you know this?). The metal of the ship conducts thought. We make our disks from it.

Paul got a picture of woolly mammoths crossing an ice sheet, pursued by bearded hunters with pale skin and head hair. He recognized the constellations undistorted not by distance from Earth but by distance backward in time.

You see, Po-wul, we are of the same people.

(I had begun to think so). Paul wondered how much of this SheuXe had known or guessed, that sly old fox with his master plan.

The genetic material is plastic. It drifts in the soup of its own stochastic processes. It reacts to outside influences—radiation, starlight, heat, anything that can alter the genome. I am tired now, Powul. We have much to do together. You come, you bring hope. You will be a great medicus here. You will bring your people—

—Paul had a picture of Tynan and Licia walking away, he fondling her, she reaching up to kiss him—

—together because you have more wisdom than the rest of them. We will protect you, because you are like us. You are we. We are you. We have failed here and you have failed there, but the very fact that you reached us here means there is hope. You have brought us a great news and a great joy, Po-wul. Thank you.

Dauli held up a shiny copper disk on a leather thong and, with great dignity, laid it on Paul's chest. Then Dauli withdrew. Paul began to feel the hypnotic spell lift. He longed to sit up and put the disk around his neck. No longer alone. No longer despoused. No longer nothing. And still a citizen of the galaxy. For they'd owned the stars once, and they would do so again.

Ongka approached. "Now you understand, Po-wul. Touch my disk and look once more into my mind." Paul did so; saw again the clockwork. Ongka smiled. His range was fractional compared with the vastness of Dauli's. Ongka was no more than a technician. Paul saw an image of Ongka sweating as he worked on the innards of a thousand-year-old stone rocket guidance system by gaslight in the underground rooms of the space center. After the rockets were launched, they briefly-illuminated the entire city and eclipsed the night. Then they flew out to sea, to a very specific region where Ongka directed them. A year later, when the celebration was to begin anew, the tides would bring back the spent, green-garlanded, barnacle-crusted rocket bodies. Then, feverishly, the technicians worked to restore the rockets for the celebration.

As the hypnosis faded, Paul realized sadly that Dauli himself comprehended almost nothing of the city's vast blueprint of titanic stone machinery powered by the wind, the sun, and the hydraulic forces of the tides. The vision contained in Dauli came from telepathic sources buried within the ancient spaceship, whose floor now served as the assembly point for fantasy rockets. Each technician had a metal disk on which were imprinted telepathic instructions on how to accomplish a specific job. No wonder that a stone age man like Ongka could know the order of the heavens or how to repair a rocket guidance system, without actually understanding astronomy or physics or engineering. No wonder they had not really bothered to dig out the mounds or to rediscover the wheel. The mounds were their collective bad memory of the last days of Avamish. To open them would be to confront the dead buried there, butchered during the worst of the rioting and warfare, when science had become reviled and feared.

The ground thundered as Paul drifted off to sleep, and another of Dauli's rockets sought its target in the gray, churning, fishy night sea.

41. New World—Year 3301

Paul was alone in a plain room half filled with sunlight, half with shadow. It did not matter where he was—Avamish, Aerie, Venice by a canal, alien city under alien sky—as he gazed lazily under the shade, through the window, at an odd assortment of walls outside, with vines growing in circles and softening harsh man-made lines. He felt whole and healthy again, cleansed of all bad memories. Dauli had healed his soul. The pain of Krings and Licia and Gregory and Nancy was only a dull knowledge now, truth, then a wink of sadness and acceptance and moving on.

A door opened and closed. He took his gaze from trying to puzzle the angles and vines outside, and looked toward the door. Auska stepped close, carrying a bucket and a sponge. "Alo, you," she said brightly. She pointed to a wooden stool in the middle of the room. "Sit, you."

He laughed, and she smiled at him. Pert, fearless, tender, loving.

He stripped his filthy jumpsuit off and sat bare-ass on the stool. He wore only his copper disk. She wrinkled her nose. "Moniam bilthy. Moniam bestibo." Humor twinkled around her eyes.

He groaned luxuriantly as she ran the hot sponge slowly and sensuously over his skin. He relaxed his elbows on his knees and stared down between his legs at the floor. A silvery puddle grew on the stone tiles. It didn't matter. The afternoon wore on as she hummed to herself, sponging him down. They stared into one another's eyes, and kept staring, evidently not able to see enough of each other.

He tried to recognize in her facial beauty somehow a composite of earth phenotypes, now that the thought made sense, and thought she might walk unnoticed somewhere in one of the ancient cities—either in the Orient, because of the almondness of her eyes, or among tall and slender Africans because of her dusky skin, or in northern Europe because of the squareness of her features and because of the short silvery hair that looked platinum blonde. He recalled the bizarre and life-threatening ritual of the pale-skinned Europeans, before people had known better, to stew in deadly sunlight for days at a time to activate their melanin and make their skin as dark as possible.

She finished bathing him and peeled off her clothes. Her skirt dropped to the floor, and her sling top. She was slender and lovely, with smooth skin the color of plums. Paul noted details—the innie belly button, the flax-white hair in the Y of her pudenda, the glistening blue nipples with their swollen aureoles—as he drank her in with his eyes. Her gaze was were full of hunger for him.

She sat on the stool and he knelt beside her. In slow motions, savoring every second, he alternately dunked the sponge in the warm water and then ran it down her sides. He stared as the water gleamed on her young skin, then ran down in a trickle into her fine waist and over her bottom. She raised her arms as he reached around to sponge her belly, her breasts, from behind, and embraced her. She turned, taking him into her arms. Together, still wet, they fell upon the bed and made passionate love. They were one and the same people, separated by fifty thousand years, the same amount of genetic drift—people on Earth had come from somewhere, from the stars, perhaps from a crashed ship as on N60A. They were faster, smarter, better, maybe meaner and more ruthless than Neanderthal. They spread out quickly over the planet during a 100,000 year period. They began to mutate due to genetic drift. Then came the age of exploration, of empire, when quick travel and instant communication fused them back together in a final amalgam.

He was now a great medicus of her people. No more spousing here. They would be husband and wife. By her ardor, she showed how desirable he was. He, in turn, had been hungry for a long time and now he had found a wonderful food. They rocked together, slapped against each other, shook the old wooden bed until it creaked in rhythm with his thrusting, her long legs sprawled over his shoulders as his body became a machine and slammed rapidly and repeatedly against her, and she writhed, she held her arms behind her head and closed her eyes and moaned in ecstasy.

He remembered a dream he'd had, of a girl riding by on a horse. It was Auska. How could he have known back then? Oh, but he had secretly wanted her all along. The girl rode through the forest without saying a word. Birds could be heard twittering brightly in all of their mating calls. Paul followed the girl and the horse. For a moment he lost sight of them around a bend. He hurried and came to a river. The horse was riderless, slowly walking away on the other side of the river. The girl's cloak lay on this side, half in the mud, half in water. He knelt by the water and looked inside. There she was, spreading her arms and legs for him. Sunlight ran around her features in sparkles. He thrust himself head-first into the water and embraced her. She closed her eyes, rolled her eyes up, smiled in ecstasy as he claimed her for himself. River water streamed over her features as her smile merged with the brightness of the reflected sun. They breathed under the water, which was one of the many invincible strengths of their love. He planted his legs apart to steady himself in the stream. She let herself float as he pulled her to him. Her ankles, her calves, slid around his waist. She bent her legs to pin herself to him with her knees around his hips. He pulled her close to him, felt the satisfaction as his hardness slipped into her soft place, and they made love, again and again. Like the twin moons over Avamish, they had found each other, and for all eternity they would never let each other go.

42. New World—Year 3301

They sat in the kitchen of Dauli's house: Dauli, his old wife, Auska, Paul, Ongka, Ping Weng, Meiling Weng, Amda. The Wengs had arrived from the north with a caravan of natives who were late for the festival. They were just in time for the last night of it.

The Storybook Festival was over, for yet another year as N60 (New Sol to the human pioneers) presided over N60A's ellipsis of seasons among the moons, planets, and cosmic litter of this solar system.

The kitchen was almost an urban room. It had a small kiln built somewhat like a stove. There was a sink, with running water that could be turned on or off with a stone tap. They all sat around the kitchen table and ate from a platter of wrapped leaves. They had either spring water or watered down wine to drink.

First it was Paul's turn to tell of all that had happened, while the natives and the Wengs listened. Then the Wengs told their story. They were a close couple, and spoke in turns, each completing the other's thought:

"We had a good landing—"

"—but far north of here. Our lifeboat—"

"—is intact. Yes, maybe we could use it one day to reach Moon II—"

"—then we could figure out a mass accelerator to shoot bits of metal toward the planet."

"—we did some tests and found out that the people here are genetically identical to us. We are the same race. We can—"

"—we can interbreed and have children."

To which Paul said: "We've already taken the first step."

"What about Tynan and Licia?" Meiling asked delicately, showing sensibility toward his feelings.

"They will be safe at Akha," Paul said. "In time we'll get everything sorted out. Where we'll live."

"That's right," Ping said with a laugh, "it's just details from here on in. "

"Details," Meiling agreed. "We made it."

That night was the last night of the festival. Nearby was the building of giant statues. Ongka and Paul and Auska stood with Dauli on the top remaining floor of Dauli's apartment building. A broken wall formed a parapet over which they could lean to watch as fiery smoky rockets thundered up toward the stars.

Dauli put his hand on Paul's shoulder and fingered his own disk. No doubt he wondered how many more years he would live to see this festival. Moniam bestibo. Dauli's eyes looked wet. Probably he was sad that he would not live to see what the two kinds of humans together could accomplish.

Then city's rocket show was over. The last of the rocket flamed up, exploding over the horizon. Dauli made a gesture with his hand, back and forth, then down. Auska translated: "Kfinish," she said in Avamishan-accented Aerie pidgin, "allobah."

"Allobah," Paul imitated, squeezing her. He said with a laugh: "You're inventing a new language. Avanglomish."

The festival shifted to the hillside, as the villagers released their own stored rockets. Paul and Auska held each other as the little imitation rockets rattled more like fireworks over the skyline. Unperturbed stars flickered in the immense black universe.

On the distant hillside, hundreds of torches danced amid the night. Carts roared down the post road loaded with wine-drunk men laughing and yelling. The faint piping and drumming of the accompanying dance breathed upward to the watchers on the parapet. Dauli wiped another tear away. The air rattled with explosions, and the ground shook every time a large one blew.

Paul studied the darkness where the launch pads were. He said softly to nobody in particular: "We're not here to conquer. And we've survived. We have accomplished our mission. The people who sent us would be proud if they knew all this." As another explosion shook the city, and Auska squealed with shock, Paul held her tightly to him. He added with grim satisfaction: "God, how terrified the lizards must be tonight!"

= *Fin* =

Author Info

John T. Cullen, a San Diego Author
More info about all this on my webplex. See:
www.sandiegoauthor.com
and
www.johntcullen.com
among other sites on my webplex online.
======

I've been online a quarter century (since 1996) and continue building a webplex of thematically linked websites.

For this story, and many others I have written, please visit the Clocktower Books website at www.clocktowerbooks.com.

Seventy+ novels, short stories, and poetry collections can be found linked on my webplex online

Other features include my online shopping mall, with stylish Citta Moda (www.cittamoda.com) and more stuff coming. I also showcase all things Paris and Parisian at my Paris Bookshop (www.parisbookshop.com) so please do visit. There is a lot to browse, and you can support the effort by buying something through the affiliate retail links online.

Thanks, and enjoy the reading!

Sample My Work Online:

Read over a million words of my fiction, nonfiction, and poetry *free* at

www.galleycity.com

Read Half Free/Try-Buy. Best deal in town.
No obligation, no tracking, no data, no cookies, not even a breath mint.

Read-a-Latte.
If you decide you like it and want to see how it ends (read the whole book), you can buy the e-book (Kindle) online for the price of a cup of coffee. The coffee is gone in minutes, but the book is yours forever. I've been an Amazon affiliate in good standing for over twenty years, so you're in good hands.

It's the Bookstore Metaphor.
Think of it this way. In most bookstores, you can sit and read free as long as you want. You just can't take the book along when you leave, without first paying for it. Most samples offered online (including Amazon) reveal only the first several pages. My decades of experience leave me feeling totally at ease with having thousands of readers at Galley City 24/7.

Most of my longer works are available in both e-book and print editions. You can also order from Barnes & Noble and most other brick & mortar stores.

Happy Reading!

Read more about my work at Caffeine Books:

www.caffeinebooks.com

About Clocktower Books

Our excellent authors past and present include SF author (Pushcart Prize nominee) A. L. Sirois; Renee Horowitz (*Pharmacy Sleuth Trilogy*); Robin Marchesi (*A Small Journal of Heroin Addiction*, a poetic autobiography in a post-Beat tradition); Deborah Cannon (*Raven Trilogy*); and others including teenage novelist/poet yours truly (*moi*). To learn about our latest offerings, please visit the website at

www.clocktowerbooks.com

Clocktower Books, a pioneering Internet, e-book, and San Diego small press publisher, launched in April 1996 by publishing the world's first entire (not partial) proprietary (not public domain) novels (long works, industry standard) for reading online in HTML format (not for reading on portable media like CD-ROM, floppies, or other intermediary media). Some reviewers are confused and think Gutenberg did this first, but Gutenberg specialize in public domain. We were the first (John Argo: *Neon Blue, This Shoal of Space, Pioneers*; John T. Cullen: *CON2: The Generals of October*) to publish proprietary novels before e-commerce, during the genesis of e-book and online publishing.

Clocktower Books Museum Site

You will find at the Museum Pages (ever a work in progress) on our webplex a detailed history of our pioneering publishing ventures starting 1996.

www.museum.fyi

From 1998 to 2007, Clocktower Books also published what was, during its decade-long run, the world's first professional Web-only (online) magazine of speculative and dark fiction (or SFFH). See our entry in the SF Encyclopedia under Far Sector SFFH. Visit our Museum for full info.

We published new authors as well as officers and top names of the Science Fiction Writers of America (SFWA); more on our pioneering work at the Science Fiction Encyclopedia online (look under Far Sector).

Our magazine's major names over the years included Deep Outside SFFH and Far Sector SFFH. We published many nominees or later awardees of the Hugo, Nebula, Sturgeon, and other global awards including British, Canadian, and Australian. The leading SF magazine historian Mike Ashley (Liverpool University Press) has stated he will recognize our pioneering magazine in the final volume of his authoritative SF magazine histories.

Selected Titles by John T. Cullen

Suspense & Thrillers writing as John T. Cullen
www.onthrillerstreet.com

Novels and short stories.
Read more about my work at Caffeine Books:
www.caffeinebooks.com

NOVELS INCLUDE:

- Lethal Journey 1892 true crime/famous ghost legend at the Hotel del Coronado near San Diego; my best seller; see **Nonfiction Dead Move** for scholarly analysis on which this novel is closely and accurately based.
- CON2: The Generals of October (a Constitution Thriller;
- Siberian Girl: historical fiction spanning World War Two and the Cold War;
- Orbital Sniper: near-future techno thriller, 21st Century James Gray; his women (not 'girls') mostly have Ph.D., black belts, personalities, and important careers.
- Valley of Seven Castles, a Luxembourg Thriller: a huge thriller, homage to Robert Ludlum (Bourne Identity), and John Buchan (1915 archetype 39 Steps);
- Neon Blue, history's first HTML novel as I call it. Suspense Mystery/Thriller.

Nonfiction Books and Articles

Writing as John T. Cullen
www.readnonfiction.com/

Read more about my work at Caffeine Books:
www.caffeinebooks.com

- Dead Move: The Haunting Mystery of Kate Morgan and the Hotel del Coronado; my scholarly analysis solving the long-ago mystery of a tragic crime that drew national attention in 1892, leaving a famous ghost legend. From this info, I also wrote a historical novel Lethal Journey.
- Sator Enigma: Ancient Roman Enigma Solved At Last
- Exogravitation: Dark Energy is No More
- Seeking Helen, Finding Homer (release to be announced)
- The God Page: We Are All Animists ...and more.

Journalism and scholarship are in my soul. I hold a B.A. in Liberal Arts from the University of Connecticut (English, Comparative Lit/Classics, Languages); a second B.A. in Computer Information Systems and Accounting (my 'practical degree'), and an M.S. in Business Administration (Boston University). I was a professional writer by age 17 (summer interne reporter, The New Haven Journal-Courier daily CT metro newspaper), a published poet by age 18, and a novelist by age 19 when I completed Summer Planets as a sophomore at UConn. When it comes to nonfiction, I stick with facts and avoid conspiracies etc. Dead Move is deeply researched (by me & hotel's official historian), and Lethal Journey is carefully crafted as a robust thriller closely based on Dead Move.

SF Series Empire of Time

Writing as John Argo
www.empireoftime.com

Read more about my work at Caffeine Books:
www.caffeinebooks.com

NOVELS INCLUDE:

- <u>Summer Planets</u>, my teenage novel completed at 19; a lifetime's work in the Empire of Time series is based on it.
- <u>Blue Princess: The Storybook Planet</u> (age c23)
- <u>Mars the Divine</u>
- <u>Orwell in Orbit 2084</u>
- <u>Lantern Road</u>
- <u>Runners: Escape from Prison Planet or Die</u>
- <u>Far Wars</u>
- …and more, spanning a million years and a vast empire of time and space that is only beginning to reveal its powerful secrets with each new story. At least two unconnected short stories, <u>Harps</u> and <u>Night Songs at Um</u>, are integral to the canon.

SF Series DarkSF

Writing as John Argo
www.darksf.com

Read more about my work at Caffeine Books:
www.caffeinebooks.com

NOVELS INCLUDE:

- Doom Spore San Diego
- Meta4City
- YANAPOP (Run for Your Life, a Love Story)
- Streamliners
- Robinson Crusoe 1,000,000 A.D.
- Nebula Express
- This Shoal of Space
- …and more

What is DarkSF?

DarkSF is not gory, splatter, juvenile, or scary. Rather, like the great movies Blade Runner and Inception or the stories of Ray Bradbury, Jorge Luis Borges, or James Tiptree, Jr. (to name a handful of many great examples) DarkSF is artful, rich, atmospheric, beautiful fiction. I like to call it

The Dark Chocolate of SFFH

DarkSF can span multiple genres; most of mine is SF. An exception would be my dark holiday fantasy (Ray Bradbury wrote me a personal rave note) The Christmas Clock.

Short Stories (SFFH, Suspense)

Writing as John Argo and John T. Cullen
www.galleycity.com

Read more about my work at Caffeine Books:
www.caffeinebooks.com

ANTHOLOGIES INCLUDE:

- Night Shots (suspense/mystery/thriller)
- Strange Doors (Weird Tales/DarkSF)
- …and more

Other Works by John T. Cullen*

Including 400+ Poems and Romantic Fiction
www.galleycity.com

Read more about my work at Caffeine Books:
www.caffeinebooks.com

WORKS INCLUDE:

- <u>On Saint Ronan Street</u>, a melancholy, French-style love story written at 27 while stationed as a young U.S. Army soldier in West Germany; set in a New England college town, with strong nods to John Updike; and film <u>The Umbrellas of Cherbourg</u>.
- <u>Cymbalist Poems,</u> one of several poetry anthologies.
- <u>Paris Affaire</u>, a much later (in my 60s) cloned from <u>On Saint Ronan Street</u>, but set in Paris and with a radically different ending.
- …and more

*My birth name (European-U.S.) is Jean Thomas Cullen. As a U.S. Army brat born in Nürnberg, FRG I was named after my two grandfathers—one Luxembourgeois, the other U.S.. I find it fun and convenient to hop back & forth among the various pseudonym possibilities this opens up.

www.ingramcontent.com/pod-product-compliance
Lightning Source LLC
Chambersburg PA
CBHW020127180626
46810CB00004B/1435